A TIME FOR FIRE

....

BOOK THREE: THE MARINE LETSCO TRILOGY

PAM B. NEWBERRY

Pam B. Newberry

J. K. Brooks Publishing, LLC
WYTHEVILLE, VIRGINIA

Copyright © 2015 by Pam B. Newberry.

All rights reserved. No part of this publication may be reproduced, distributed or transmitted in any form or by any means, including photocopying, recording, or other electronic or mechanical methods, without the prior written permission of the publisher, except in the case of brief quotations embodied in critical reviews and certain other noncommercial uses permitted by copyright law. For permission requests, write to the J. K. Brooks Publishing, LLC, addressed "Attention: Permissions Coordinator," at the address below.

J. K. Brooks Publishing, LLC
177 Stone Meadow Lane
Wytheville, VA 24382
http://jkbrookspublishing.com

Publisher's Note: This is a work of fiction. Names, characters, places, and incidents are a product of the author's imagination. Locales and public names are sometimes used for atmospheric purposes. Any resemblance to actual people, living or dead, or to businesses, companies, events, institutions, or locales is completely coincidental.

Book Cover Design ©2015 Julie Kay Newberry
Book Layout ©2013 BookDesignTemplates.com

Ordering Information:
Quantity sales. Special discounts are available on quantity purchases by corporations, associations, and others. For details, contact the "Special Sales Department" at the address above.

A Time for Fire/ Pam B. Newberry. -- 1st ed.
ISBN-10: 1941061052
ISBN-13: 978-1-941061-05-3

Dedication

To Miloh — one of the best *grand-dogs* ever!

*"And glory like the phoenix midst her fires,
exhales her odours, blazes, and expires."*

–THE WORKS OF LORD BYRON

ONE

....

FIRE IN THE RAIN

By the time she arrived, Marine Letsco, Fire Marshal, observed the crowd was still gathered watching the firefighters repack their hose after knocking down the blaze. One firefighter bent and gathered up the tools that had been used to put out the structure fire. A few of the spectators pushed the boundary of the black and yellow barricade tape, their necks craned to get the best view. A gurney rolled down the side road creaking as it rumbled over the gravel. A black zipper bag was folded and ready to receive its new occupant. There was another victim. The smell didn't help.

Parking her newly acquired Chrysler Durango special service vehicle on the side street behind the Captain's car, Marine continued to survey the crowd. Two days prior, the New Brook Fire Investigations team began to suspect an arsonist was at work after they determined a sixth fire shared patterns with five others.

The rain had stopped, but water had puddled. Her right boot slipped into it before she realized she had managed to park her car in the middle of one. The murky liquid lapped up against the leather. Thankfully, I had replaced my dress shoes with my duty boots. My feet felt clunky, she thought. The lace-up boots came midway up her calf. I hope I don't stumble.

"Dang, Marine. Get your act together," she chided herself. She reached back into the vehicle to retrieve her radio and notepad. She picked up her coffee cup and took a drink. Too cold and bitter. The smell of the fire caused her to wish she had taken time to study the recent fire reports before she was summoned to this one. She knew a trait of many arsonists was to linger and watch. Marine continued to observe the crowd, as she hoped she would spy him.

It had been six months since she was promoted. The day she saw her name on her Fire Marshal badge was a proud day. When she walked into the fire investigative offices located with the Evansham Regional Bomb Squad in New Brook, Virginia, she knew she'd found her calling. Chief Fire Marshal Edwin Altizer personally assigned her to determine if the recent fires occurring in the region were related or if they were the work of multiple arsonists.

Marine looked around as she pulled the flameproof coveralls over her official blue uniform. The overalls coupled with her duty boots made her feel upholstered with all of the extra fabric. Her clunky feet felt extra heavy with the overalls strapped on the outside. She knew that when walking into a newly burned building, she didn't want her clothes getting too warm or even catching fire—the unattractive fire investigator's uniform was a necessity. It was early June—hot and humid. The walk to the building caused beads of sweat to begin to collect on her forehead.

"Letsco!" Chief Altizer called. "Where's your badge?"

She looked down and realized it was under the inner flap of her coveralls. *Damn. I would have to forget that now when he's watching me.*

"Are you ready to go in, Letsco?"

"Yes, sir."

"Good. Now, let's see what you can tell us about our arsonist."

What a hard ass, she thought. But, he is the Chief. I'm going to have to prove myself to him every day. It doesn't matter how good a firefighter I was. I am a woman, and I am going to have to show him I can pull my weight as a fire marshal. Somehow, though, I doubt I can walk in these boots through this muck and grime.

As she stepped, she could feel her feet slip and slide. The floor had some kind of goo covering it.

Fire Marshal Tom Willard was taking pictures of a wall. His back was to her. He stood with a broad stance, his feet positioned to steady himself, yet she saw his feet slide as he tried to stand still.

"What's on the floor, Tom?"

"Evidently, this was a candy store. We're walking on melted sugar mixed with the water, what most people call syrup."

"Oh, what a mess."

"Indeed. The body was in the back storage room. I believe this was the point of origin. If so, the poor man had no chance to get out of here. See how the fire went straight up this wall? The arsonist knew what he was doing when he set this one. This makes five deaths and seven fires. It's not even Wednesday yet. This guy is diabolical."

"But, do we know if it is a man, or even if the fires are done by the same person? We are just now making the connection that the fires could be related. Right?"

"You weren't in the office when we got the call from the Chief. He said that your review of the series of fires in Salem had pointed out some similarities to the fires we'd been working. The theory is you were right to connect them. Because of your suspicions, the main brass thinks this arsonist is a guy and he is trying to copy the cult arsonist, Thomas Sweatt."

"Really? But, how would our arsonist know about Sweatt? He's been in prison a while."

"Evidently, there has been a lot written about him. His story is all over the Internet."

"Well, he did use simplistic methods to start fires. And, the fires we've seen this week seemed to fit that same approach. Any ideas what this guy used here?"

"Yes. Another simplistic method. Everyday objects. But, like all of his other fires, he wanted the blaze to grow fast. Sweatt didn't work like that. That was why his fires took a long time to connect to each other. This guy is consistent in his style. It is his methods that change, but they are simple. At least, so far they are."

Marine heard a clamor. She turned and saw the paramedics were pushing the gurney toward them.

"Can I see?"

"He's crispy."

"Let me see."

The body of the owner of the candy shop was in a frozen state and very brittle. The paramedics, in order to carefully move his body onto the gurney and not lose any small fragments from the skull, had wrapped the top of his head in plastic cling-wrap. Marine studied his face. Sadly, he probably knew what was happening as he died. His mouth was still open from apparent screaming. I looked at the rest of the body. He was in the classic fighter's stance. All of his joints or flexor muscles had constricted. I continued looking him over for any possible signs of injury that could have been made by a weapon, nothing stood out.

"Any weapon marks?" Tom asked as he snapped photos.

"No. Just like the others. We won't know until a detailed post-mortem exam is done."

"I wonder how he is able to set the fires without the victims hearing him."

"That is a mystery. He's managed to set his fires deep in the interior of the different structures and in unlikely places of vehicles. Yet, when people were around, there were no survivors or witnesses to his deeds."

"The Chief will want to know these details. What else do you notice?"

Marine continued to study the room for a few minutes. "The fire went fast. Has anyone been able to talk with the victim's family?" Tom shook his head no. "Well, if we can pinpoint the time the fire started, we can determine if he used a lot of one particular kind of accelerant. I suspect we'll find the evidence we need as we look around."

"There you go. Look at that." Tom pointed toward a large bowl sitting on top of a class counter.

Marine walked to it and looked it over carefully. It was leaning to one side.

"This bowl appears different from the other things in the store that aren't totally burned. I bet the arsonist used it to hold accelerant. He probably thought it would go up in the flames or at least be scorched to the point we'd think it belonged to the victim." Marine pulled out her cell and took a few pictures.

She picked up the bowl to examine it more closely thinking she might learn more. There was a piece of paper stuck to the bottom. She pulled it away and handed it to Tom.

He opened it up. "I was afraid it would be the same," Tom said. The look on his face told her it wasn't good.

* * * * *

Back at the office after finishing the initial walk through, Tom and Marine rifled through the pile of papers they had gathered regarding a recent series of fires. Marine pulled one folder open and slid some papers aside. She pulled out an evidence bag and handed it to Tom.

"Here. Is it there?"

"Yep. It's the same."

"Damn. How was this missed before?"

"We need to check through these others first. They all might not be related."

"It's the same arsonist. I know it. I can feel it." Marine said as she continued shoving folders aside. The piece of paper she held was an exact match to the other two samples they found.

As she pulled another evidence bag out of a third folder, she felt cold shivers run down her spine. "Look, Tom," she said placing the two pieces side-by-side.

"They are from the same box. They fit like a jigsaw puzzle."

"Wait here. You've given me an idea."

Marine found Fire Marshal Charles Massie, the Evidence Tech. They went to the evidence room that was kept locked at all times. As the evidence tech, Charles had the only key. Inside were boxes and boxes of files for fires of unknown origin that were deemed suspicious but were never confirmed to be the work of an arsonist. Marine had a feeling they were stumbling onto something big—maybe bigger than Sweatt's firebug work. She signed out four boxes and carried them back to the processing lab, located next door. She walked down the hall and called for Tom to join her.

As he entered the room, she said, "Here, Tom. Help me find the samples from these fires. I have a feeling we're going to find pieces of that puzzle."

They began to pull the items out and laid them on the stainless steel tables making sure the boxes stayed with each pile of evidence.

Unfortunately, she was right. After their initial search, they continued to go back to the evidence room and signed out more boxes. Half the morning passed with them searching through over forty boxes going back twenty years. While they searched for the evidence, they also noted the location of the information card that was routinely stapled to the outside of the box in a plastic sheath. Marine and Tom stood back and looked at the result. There were fifteen pieces that all appeared to come from the same puzzle. The arsonist had carefully taped them to a similar style of stationary as the piece they had found at the fire scene that morning. Evidently, the arsonist taped each puzzle piece to the paper in such a manner that it could be interlocked with a companion piece. He then folded the paper and placed the paper where it could be found. Many times the paper was singed or partially burned. But, all were found in the evidence boxes. Now, the pieces were a complete puzzle.

"I wonder how many didn't survive a fire?" Tom asked as Marine surveyed the evidence.

"Somehow, the ones we have here were placed in these boxes. No one has made the connection before that the puzzle pieces were a message from an arsonist. How is that possible?"

"I don't know. I'd never found a puzzle piece at any of my investigations until the one I saw three days ago. That's the reason I reacted the way I did back at the fire scene when I saw the paper taped under the bowl."

"Let's categorize what we have here. We need to determine how long this particular signature has been showing up," Marine reached for her notepad. "You call out the dates of the fires, names of the investigators, and the disposition of the case from the log call stapled to the box. We'll only look at the boxes where we found puzzle pieces. I'll log it here."

After about thirty minutes, they had a list of twenty-five fires dating back twenty years. Two fire investigators listed had worked two fire scenes each that included puzzle pieces. One was listed as retired while the other was deceased. The remaining ten fires were at different stages of investigation since they had occurred within the past two weeks.

"Tom. Twenty years. And no one made a connection. This is mind boggling."

"You've got to remember, we didn't have a strong fire investigative department until about five years ago. It's only been in the last two years that we've added full-time secretarial staff. Up until then, I didn't have someone who could help me with organization. I was lucky to get my notes transcribed before I forgot what my shorthand meant. With budget cuts coming down this year, we may be heading backwards instead of forward with hiring the support we need."

"Hey, Tom and Letsco." Fire Marshal Matt Pike walked into the processing room.

"You were out on an investigation?" Marine asked as she moved a box to another table.

"Yep. Fremont Street. It was a car fire. Thankfully, no one was injured."

"Sorry to hear about your ex-wife being in the hospital. How is she?" Tom asked as he took the top off a box and reached inside.

"She'll recoup."

"Oh, good. I hadn't heard the details. What exactly happened?" Tom said as he marked another column.

"She fell down the steps."

"How'd that happen?" Marine inquired moving the last box.

"She tripped over the vacuum cleaner. I told her housework would kill her. She hadn't cleaned the house in weeks. I had to reintroduce her to the vacuum cleaner the other day. I guess she forgot how to use it. She called me over and asked me to show her. Go figure."

Marine started to reply but thought better of it. The smirk on his face didn't add to his lack of manners.

"What are you two doing?" Matt said as he picked up an evidence bag.

"We found an interesting piece of evidence at an earlier fire scene. It gave Marine an idea. So, we're in here making a record of a link we think makes all of these fires connected," Tom said as he put the lid back on his box.

"Look what I found at my fire scene." The evidence bag Matt held up made our findings increase by one. "Why would someone tape a puzzle piece to a piece of paper? You know, I found two more just like this last month."

Marine's mouth ran dry. "Really? Where did you put those?"

"They're in my desk with my other files. I hadn't had a chance to finalize my paperwork and place them in the evidence boxes. You want me to get them?" Marine nodded yes. "I'll get them in a minute. You know, it's odd someone would do that. I do that when I've lost a puzzle piece and find it later. I'll tape it to some stationary so I won't lose it. But, I always put it back into the box that I think it belongs to. Guess a lot of people are working puzzles and losing their pieces."

Marine looked at Tom. How did this guy become a fire marshal, she wondered. Looking at Matt more closely, she noticed that he was handsome, but his hair should have been blonde instead of the red hair with gray specs starting to show. She reasoned he dyed it to hide his blonde. His approach wasn't very successful.

She looked back at what they had gathered. There were over twenty-three puzzle pieces placed on the evidence tables. She knew they had an active serial arsonist that had been working for some time. The job of finding him had just begun.

TWO

RANDLE THE CANDLE

One day they will call me Randall the Candle, Pat Pike said to himself as he prepared another puzzle piece. His twin brother, Matt, was such a fool. Even as kids, Pat managed to set Matt up to take the fall for his arson fires. The judge didn't know what he was talking about when he put me in juvie. Hell, I was only ten for Christ's sake, Pat thought as he folded the stationary just right. I'm going to fix them all, but especially Matt. He could have served time for me. He didn't have to cry like a little baby and tell everyone he was innocent. Pat slammed the paper down on the table. Besides, he should have loved me enough to understand me. Matt had no right making mommy and daddy hate me.

It was early morning. The latest fire was perfect. That old candy man never saw me until it was too late. He chuckled. Alone in the house in Salem, Pat knew no one would know he was inside. Pat walked over to the cot he'd placed at the far wall of the den. He laid down and put his head on his pillow, cuddled up against the wall, and tried to rock himself to sleep. He was restless. He jumped up, walked into the kitchen, and turned on the TV.

"I'm taking your identity, Dave Randall. Pat Pike no longer exists after tonight," Pat said to the lifeless body sitting on the bench propped against the wall. "I told you when I broke in here that I knew all about you. I told you not to give me any lip. Not that you would have lived much longer. But, I rather liked telling you my plans. Now, I'll just have to talk to you, and this time, you won't be talking back." Pat walked over to Dave and looked him over closely.

"You're not stinking yet. But, I'll do away with you properly just as soon as I figure out what I'm going to do next. It was my good fortune—" Pat stopped mid-sentence, laughed aloud, and then stopped and stared. "I guess it is my fortune now. You made all kinds of arrangements to be a recluse. But, you didn't count on Jack Manytoes meeting up with me when he got arrested. Jack told me all about your way of living. Your fortune is now my fortune, Mr. Dave. You made a mistake in not letting people see you. When Jack told me I looked a lot like you, it gave me the idea to take your place after I broke out of that prison. Prison for the criminally insane," he scoffed. "Crazy. I'll show them crazy. Crazy like a fox."

"I remember the look in your eyes the night I broke in here. You thought I was some hired help you'd gotten to clean the other side of your house. You were crazy with fear that I was going to rob you. You were right. I did. Now, look at you. Sitting there all pretty with that gaping hole in your chest. You should have been deathly afraid of me. One day, my brother will be just as afraid of me. I'm going to see to that. He thinks he is so smart being a Fire Marshal. Hell, he doesn't even know how to start a fire. He's such a pansy ass. I wonder what he'd say if he could see me now, living here in this mansion of yours.

"Dave, I will tell you this much, you were smart. Very smart to get a nice place off the beaten path." Pat stopped and looked over at the TV. "Hey, Dave. Do you see that? Look at that. They have my latest fire on the TV news. Oh, and look there. It's that Letsco lady. You know the one I told you about, the new fire investigator that works with Matt. I'm going to make their lives a living inferno before I'm done. They won't know what hit them." Pat started to laugh again and began to dance a jig around the room.

After spending a few minutes watching the news, Pat danced across the room to the sink. "You know, Dave," Pat called back as he put some water in the teakettle. "You were wise to divide this house and make it into two different homes. No one has seen you in over fifteen years. That is so clever. I mean I can come in here and take your place and there is no one, except Jack, who would know I'm not you. Let's see," Pat said as he looked at the calendar. "According to this here calendar I convinced you to make after I cut off your left thumb, starting tomorrow you will have six people here working on the other side of the house—cleaning it, restocking the kitchen with fresh food, and servicing your car. That means we'll move over to the unoccupied part of the house tomorrow night. I'll have four weeks to figure out what to do with your body before they come on this side of the house to clean and get it ready for me to move back over. In the meantime, I'll work out a wicked plan I can hatch for my blameless brother and that long-legged, haughty wench, Marine."

* * * * *

Three weeks passed. Pat moved Dave to the other side of the house. He managed to venture out into Salem, strike more arson fires, and began the groundwork of framing Matt. He even made several trips to the New Brook Fire Investigation and Evansham Regional Bomb Squad offices. One trip was extra beneficial. He not only stole one of Matt's uniforms, but he had an unexpected treat while walking down the hallway not far from Matt's desk. He thought back to that moment—

"Matt. I thought you weren't coming in today. I guess you couldn't stay away with all of these arson fires we've been having, could you?" Pat looked up and couldn't believe his eyes. It was Marine.

He moved his hand over his lips to help muffle and disguise his voice. "Yep. Can't seem to get enough of this place."

"We're all going down to Belle's tonight, can you come?"

"Sure." Pat continued walking out with a purpose.

Marine called after him, "See you there!"

Pat waved at her and walked on out.

That was one piece of fine acting and she's dumber than he thought. She never had a freaking clue it was me. And, it gave me a new idea, he thought as he walked into the pantry, opened up the freezer chest, and looked at Dave's body.

"It's time, Dave. I've finally figured out what we need to do together. It will be so much fun. You're going to die all over again, but this time the freaking authorities, along with my guiltless brother and stupid Marine, will think it is me and not you. I can't believe how perfect this will be."

* * * * *

Pat finished preparing Dave for his final trip to the cabin.

"You know, Dave. These last three weeks since I decided to switch places with you have proven to be very interesting. Ever since I found the cabin, owned by Jack Manytoes' family—my cellmate—I've been making lots and lots of plans. It's a shame you can't see the place where you're going to die again. There's got to be six or seven hundred acres around this cabin. It looks like this cabin hasn't been used for years. Way back there in the national forest. It's perfect." Pat continued pulling out Dave's teeth as he thought about the day he came upon the cabin not long after he had escaped from the prison for the criminally insane. The cabin was run down and deserted. But, the location was isolated and perfect for his plan. It was an old moonshiner's place complete with an escape tunnel and a grown over path that led down to the main road where the moonshiners could haul out their shine.

Before Pat put his plan into play with Dave, he cleaned out the cabin, checked out the tunnel, which was a perfect escape route, and made sure the path was cleared of any debris. Pat found a campsite about six miles up the main road from the cabin. He learned the campsite offered RV parking with four-wheelers for rent. He decided he'd keep that in mind if he needed it later. He spent a few days preparing the cabin for a planned escape if the authorities came looking. He gathered gallon glass jugs that were left in the cabin and filled some with gasoline, some with diesel fuel. He placed them around the windows with one-pound cans of black powder. Some cans he placed inside additional cans to delay their ignition. His idea was that as a fireball erupted, the cans would start exploding. It would cause a distraction and a means for him to get through the tunnel, and then off the backside of the mountain before the police would know he was gone. Then, he was even luckier. He met Dave.

He looked Dave over. All of his teeth were gone. Pat checked the ends of Dave's fingers to make sure he had not left any trace of fingerprints after removing the tips. He checked for any possible means to identify Dave, and then placed his body into a body bag that he had stolen from the Fire Investigation lab.

"You know, Jack Manytoes should have received that letter I wrote him by now. The authorities will have read how I told him I'd be breaking him out in the next day or two and taking him back to his old home place. I told him—

'I plan to break you out and get you to your family's cabin. The cabin you told me about that you used as a boy. I found it and it will be ready for you. Don't forget now. Don't tell a soul I'm coming for you.'

"The funny part, Dave, is that even if they find my hidey-hole, they won't make the connection that it was used as an escape route. You see. They will think you are me." Pat laughed evilly.

He placed Dave's body in the camper, and then made sure he had all of his supplies. If he figured correctly, the authorities should show up in the next few days. But, if not, he'd gathered provisions so he was ready to wait for them. Turning the ignition, Pat looked at the clock on the dashboard. I've got time to drop the camper off at the RV site and settle down for the night. Then, around midnight, I'll take Dave's body up to the cabin, he thought as he drove to the campsite.

* * * * *

"Well, Dave. We're here." Pat carried Dave's body and placed him inside the cabin near a pile of cardboard. "This is perfect. The fire department won't be able to get their equipment up here. I piled these stacks of cardboard, paneling, and thin sheets of wood. They should give the fire what it needs to burn extra hot."

Pat moved some things around and over Dave's body after he took him out of the body bag. "You're thawing just fine, Dave. You know, it was my luck you told me about the infrared motion sensors you had laying around your house. I added them out in the front and around back to alert me just in case I don't see the law coming up. Now, all I have to do is sit back and wait."

Pat brought enough food so if he had to stay a week or two, it wouldn't matter. He planned to not venture out of the cabin except to make an occasional appearance down at the RV camp during the day.

* * * * *

Two days passed. Pat had just come in from relieving himself. "You know, Dave. It's a shame. You'll never have the pleasure of taking a leak in the woods again. It's a beautiful—" An alarm was tripped.

Pat moved quickly. He looked out one of the windows and caught a glimpse of an officer who had stepped to the left of the big bush near the edge of the front yard. He got his shotgun, went to the door, and stepped into the doorway.

"You'll not take me alive you sons-of-bitches. I'm not going back." He shot buckshot in the direction of the officer, and then slammed the door, placed the shotgun in Dave's hands, and stopped to listen.

An officer called to him through a megaphone, "Pat Pike. We've got you surrounded. You might as well give up. Come out with your hands up. You have nowhere to go."

"Like Hell," Pat yelled. "I'll shoot the first one of you that comes in here." He maneuvered to the tunnel, gathering up his things that he would need back at the campsite. He pulled the fuse, watched the fire light off; the flames lapped up around Dave's body. He made sure that the flames were spreading as he had planned. Satisfied his fire would be an extra toasty one, he closed the concrete trap door after he slipped down into the tunnel.

Pat took his time because he knew no one would be following him. As he emerged out of the tunnel, he could hear the black powder exploding. He looked back toward the cabin and could see a lot of flames and smoke above the tops of the trees. "She's toasty indeed," Pat said.

He looked around and listened carefully. "They're not thinking of following me. They don't have a clue that I have made another great escape. With all of the explosions, those bastards are scared shitless."

Pat pulled off his fake hair and beard and his clothes. "Dressing like a Grizzly Adams look-alike will throw them off," Pat said as he placed the things into a fanny pack.

Next, he dressed in a black performance long sleeve jersey and baggy shorts with all of the related mountain bike riding gear—helmet, gloves, socks, and shoes. He had placed a Trek cross-country mountain bike near the tunnel exit and had mapped out a bike path that he had found not far from the tunnel.

"Time to ride," Pat said as he made his way down to the main road. He followed the main road for the six miles to the campground where his RV was stashed. After tying the bike on the back of the RV, he went inside, took a shower, and changed clothes again. This time, he wore his jeans and a shirt that was Dave's. He started up the RV.

"This has been a perfect day. It's time to head for the great city of New Brook. Dave's dead. Now the authorities think I'm dead. I think it's time for Matt to get himself a hooker." Pat laughed aloud, as he drove down the road.

About three miles down the road, Pat saw a rural fire truck making its way up the mountain to his fire.

"I think I will start three fires in three different areas. Got to keep those lazy firefighters busy in New Brook."

THREE

AUNT BETSY

She never liked getting her hands dirty. The death of Ana-Geliza still did not set well with her. She tried several times over the last six months to tell Marine what happened that night after Marine and Chet, her adopted nephew, went to bed. Aunt Betsy tied her apron securely, reached across the sink, and gathered up the soap. She washed her hands with solemn respect thinking about how she managed to take another life. Something she swore twenty years before she would only do in order to protect her family. Ana-Geliza gave her no choice. She had to protect Marine.

Aunt Betsy reached into the refrigerator and pulled out the dinner roll dough that was rising in her large bread bowl. She dumped it out onto the counter, slapped it hard, and again looked out her kitchen window. The late afternoon sun shone brightly on her cottage flowers. She loved her home—Trout House Falls—it always helped her feel safe. How am I, Elizabeth James Lanter, going to explain my life to Marine? I've never told her the truth about Chet, either. The screened back door opened with an audible squeak.

"Aunt Betsy. I'm so glad to catch you. Are you preparing dinner? Can you stop? I've got somewhere to take you," Marine said racing into the kitchen, placing a kiss on Aunt Betsy's cheek, and opening the refrigerator door. "Do you have any of your banana pudding stashed in here?"

"Yes. No. And, no." Aunt Betsy walked over to Marine and pushed the refrigerator door closed. "Where do you need to take me? Slow down and explain it. I'm in the midst of making my dinner rolls. I can't leave them now."

"Oh, Aunt Betsy. You must. You won't believe what I've got."

"You're right. You've got to tell me before I can believe it." She smiled. She had come to love Marine and hoped she loved her, too. Aunt Betsy worried she could lose her.

A Time for Fire

"They gave me my new Durango special service vehicle. We've been working so many fire scenes lately; you've not had a chance to check it out. But, man, it is sweet. Come on. You can stop for a few minutes and go for a ride in it." Marine pulled at her and guided her toward the door.

Aunt Betsy pulled her arm out of her grasp and said, "Now, wait a minute, little girl. You can wait on me. If that's all, you have in mind. I can get these rolls ready for rising. You grab yourself some tea, and I think I might be able to find you some banana pudding. But, you have to sit down there. You can eat it while I fix my rolls. You are staying for dinner, aren't you?"

"Yes, of course, I wouldn't miss your famous rolls. What else are you having?"

"Well, I thought I'd make Vida's meatloaf, Italian green beans, and mashed potatoes. The beans I picked out of the garden this morning, so they are extra special. You remember Vida, don't you?"

"I remember you talking about her. She was a neighbor?"

"Yes. A good friend. She's been gone a few years now. She gave me that recipe and told me not to tell a soul. So, I promised I wouldn't. I named the recipe after her so I wouldn't be lying." Marine laughed. "Now, here's your banana pudding. While you eat, I need to tell you some things about me and my past."

Marine looked up. A serious look crossed her face. "Are you okay? I mean health wise?"

"Yes. I'm not baring my soul because I'm dying. Nothing like that. I have decided it is time I tell you a few things about myself. So, you sit and eat. I will talk. Okay?"

"Okay."

Aunt Betsy watched Marine place the bowl of banana pudding in front of her like a hungry bear positioning a beehive ready to devour the honey.

"I had no idea I was so hungry," Marine said. "This pudding is just divine. One day you need to tell me how you make it."

"Better. I'll have you make it and I'll supervise. Now. You eat. I'll talk." Aunt Betsy began shaping the rolls, making sure they were properly placed on her baking sheet to give the right amount of space so that the rolls would rise just right. "I have a lot to tell you. It is probably best that you don't interrupt me so that I don't lose my place." She smiled at

Marine. She hoped Marine would understand and still love her as she did now. It was a risk she had to take.

"I'm ready when you are," Marine said. She took another bite, "I must say this is so silky and creamy, and the fresh vanilla flavor is luscious." Aunt Betsy sat down.

"I guess I just have to say it and we'll go from there. I told you that once I worked for the Bureau of INR—intelligence and research—within the Department of State. The INR was tasked with analyzing information as it came in from other departments and agencies of the government, such as the FBI, CIA, and even agencies, such as NASA."

Marine continued eating but nodded. She looked at Aunt Betsy as if to say go on.

"What I'm about to tell you, for the most part, is now public knowledge, but you may not have heard much about the INR. I began working for the Bureau in 1942 as an agent. The INR was originally formed as the research and analysis branch of the Office of Strategic Services. As an agent, I worked in that aspect of the Bureau until 1945 when it was transferred to the Department of State at the end of WWII where the Bureau of INR became an important part of the U.S. Intelligence. As an inactive agent, I do not know the current number of employees, which is classified. I share all of this so that you understand my knowledge and background with special services and intelligence, and, as a result, I was privileged to know about the work you used to do as an assassin with TRANS."

Marine looked up with caution. She looked around the room.

"What?" Aunt Betsy asked. "You expecting Chet to jump out and say 'surprise,' or something?"

"Kind of."

"He won't. I'm sharing facts. Hard facts."

"Why didn't—"

"Not now. Let me continue. Are you ready for more?" Marine nodded.

Aunt Betsy placed the rolls on a nearby counter. She covered them with damp cloths and turned to Marine. "What I'm about to tell you now I need to explain. It is important. You must wait until I finish."

"Okay."

"The night of the explosion, when you rescued me from Ana-Geliza, I told you and Chet that I was going to sleep in your apartment out back because it was easier for me to get around with my hurt leg. Do you remember?" Marine nodded her head again. "I lied. I have a secret hiding place where I keep some of my gear from my agent days. I went out there and waited until Chet had left and I was sure you had gone to sleep. I then left the house and went to where I knew Ana-Geliza was hiding. She had taken me there when she first kidnapped me. Ana-Geliza did not expect me. We had a confrontation. I eliminated her, and then I did away with her body."

"You what? WHAT?"

"During my confrontation with Ana-Geliza, she revealed things about TRANS and Aunt Jeannie even I didn't know."

"TRANS? Aunt Jeannie? WHAT?" Marine stood up.

"Marine. You have to let me get this out so you have the full picture. Okay?"

"Okay, but it's hard." Marine sat back down.

"I understand. First, let me explain Aunt Jeannie. Though you know her from your training days, she and I were at one time best of friends. We both worked at INR together in the early days. We jokingly began calling each other Aunt after a case we worked on together that involved these little old ladies who were spinsters. It stuck after a while. There was a time when Aunt Jeannie decided she wanted to move on. We stayed in touch for a while, but eventually, we lost contact. Then, when Ana-Geliza told me she worked for Aunt Jeannie and that Aunt Jeannie or AJ, as she called her, owned TRANS, I knew you were in danger. Ana-Geliza told me she had been hired by AJ to kill you on the cruise. When that failed, AJ directed her to follow you here to New Brook. But, AJ didn't know I was living here." Aunt Betsy got up and refilled her iced tea glass. "Do you want more?"

Marine shook her head. "Holy Christ. Aunt Jeannie owned TRANS? And, you're saying that Ana-Geliza had stalked me the entire time? Even before I had fallen and developed amnesia?"

Aunt Betsy poured more tea and held up Marine's empty bowl as though she were asking if Marine wanted more banana pudding. Marine shook her head no.

Aunt Betsy continued, "Yes, Ana-Geliza had stalked you the entire time. She said that Aunt Jeannie wanted to be sure you were made into an example because she had learned you were planning to leave TRANS."

"How's that even possible? I didn't even know I was going to leave. I was unhappy and hated what I was doing. But, I liked the money. I felt trapped."

"Ana-Geliza said that Aunt Jeannie went crazy when she learned that you had booked the cruise to the Caribbean. She changed your trip and booked Ana-Geliza as your second so that Ana-Geliza would be able to take you out. Your fall put a crimp into their plans. I think it saved your life."

Marine sat there and looked down at her tea. She twirled the glass around rubbing the moisture off the glass with her fingers.

"What are you thinking?" Aunt Betsy asked.

"I was wondering how much of my life Aunt Jeannie had manipulated and I didn't even know. I always felt my climb at TRANS was a little off. It seemed too convenient. I felt like I was a pawn."

"You were. And, so was Ana-Geliza. I didn't want to kill again. But, I had to. When she told me that TRANS was a front and it was owned by Aunt Jeannie, I knew that the outcome of my confrontation would only end one way. I had to eliminate Ana-Geliza in order to put Aunt Jeannie in the dark. This meant that Aunt Jeannie would come here to find you. To my knowledge, she doesn't know about me. I've done a fairly good job of keeping my past secret and my current whereabouts unknown. There is only one other person that knows."

"Chet?"

"No. Drake."

"Drake? What? You have to stop shocking me like this, Aunt Betsy. You are this sweet, little old lady. Sorry, but you are. And, you can take out villains, like Ana-Geliza. You remind me of a cross between Miss Marple and Evelyn Salt, the CIA lady. You're a sleeper."

Aunt Betsy smiled.

* * * * *

The flight to Evansham had not been as bad as she had been told it would be. Getting through security was never an issue for her. She had managed to keep her security clearance badge renewed and up-to-date. She didn't have pawns strategically placed around the world for nothing. It was nice to know that her little network could work for her when she needed it.

"Thank you, Ms. AJ Bathroy. I'm sure you will enjoy your stay here in the Evansham Region. May I help you with directions?" the rental car clerk asked as she offered a broad smile.

"No. But, you could tell me about how long it takes to drive to New Brook?" Aunt Jeannie said as she placed the contract for the car inside her purse.

"About thirty minutes or so depending on traffic. You'll head south on Interstate 581. It will take you around the city of Evansham. You should enjoy the ride on this beautiful sunny day."

"I'm sure I'll enjoy a lot of things about my trip." Aunt Jeannie turned with a light step and made her way to her car.

The drive into New Brook was not bad. She drove along looking at the buildings and watching people along the main street. She pulled into the driveway of The Edith, a specialty boutique hotel. She thought she might as well stay at a nice place while she was taking care of business. Ana-Geliza hadn't contacted her for several weeks. She knew that meant something had happened. Marine would pay for the loss of a valuable employee whether she had anything to do with it or not. Ana-Geliza may have made a mistake or two, but she was a good asset. Finding a good agent was not an easy thing to do. Everyone always was out for his or her self. They never put the job first. That was Marine's problem. She wanted to have a life. Hell, no one has a life in this business. You just do what you do until you die. Well, Marine's going to enjoy her benefits in a body bag. I'm here to see to that.

Aunt Jeannie walked into the side entrance of the hotel and to the check-in counter.

"Good afternoon. Welcome to The Edith, the finest boutique hotel this side of Evansham. How may I help you?" the young lady standing behind the counter had short brown hair with attractive highlights that seemed to make her face shine. Aunt Jeannie thought she'd make someone a pretty little harlot.

"I have a reservation. The name is Jean Bathroy. I've booked a room for one night. If I find I need to stay longer, will that be possible?"

"Let me see." The clerk looked down at the computer screen. A few seconds went by. "Yes, ma'am. You may stay for up to one week if you need to. After that, we may need to move you to another room as we have a group coming in that has requested a series of rooms together."

"That's fine. When will I need to notify you of my plans?"

"The sooner, the better, but we can probably accommodate you without too much trouble if you don't mind moving rooms."

"Perfect. Now, one last question. Is there any place you might recommend I go for an early dinner? I noticed your restaurant hasn't opened yet for dinner."

"Yes, ma'am. Belle's. It is located down Main Street." The clerk pointed. "It is about mid-way down the sidewalk, in the middle of town on the right hand of the street. It is about a three to five minute walk."

"Perfect. Thank you."

After checking out her room, Aunt Jeannie made her way down to Belle's. She walked in and surveyed the restaurant. The walls were decorated with a series of photographs, the windows had cafe curtains, and the tables were wooden trimmed in blue with matching wooden chairs.

"Have a seat wherever you like, I'll be right with you," the waitress said, handing Aunt

Jeannie a menu and carrying a tray of drinks and food to a table in the corner.

Aunt Jeannie moved to a nearby table and watched the waitress work. She took special note of her appearance, as she always liked pretty, young things. This one was attractive with dark hair pulled back in a ponytail, a pleasant face with big, blue eyes. Her clothes were trimmed close to outline her slim, but curvaceous figure. Her top accentuated her well-shaped breasts and her shorts showed the strength in her legs. Aunt Jeannie thought back to when she was in her prime; she looked as good then. Yet, she knew she could use someone like her in her operation.

The waitress walked up. "Hi, I'm Belle. Have you had time to look over the menu?"

"Hi, Belle. Do you own this place?"

"Yes. I do. Is this your first time here?"

"Yes. It is my first time in town. I see you have pictures all over your walls."

"Yes. They are of the folks from around here. So, do you know what you'd like to eat or drink?"

"What do you recommend?"

"Well, we have lots of good food. The menu shows a listing of items—fried chicken, Salisbury steak, and Shepard's pie."

"Yes, but what do you like?"

"How about fried chicken, green beans, and mashed potatoes?"

"That sounds good."

"Would you want biscuits or corn bread?"

"Biscuits."

"And to drink?"

"I've heard country sweet tea is good. Bring me a glass of that. Do you mind if I look around?"

"I'll have your drink right out and feel free to look around. We like it when new folks come in here and get to know us." Belle turned and walked away, swaying her fanny at just the right pace. Aunt Jeannie made a note of her style. Very effective, she thought.

The wall to her left had the most pictures. It looked like none of them were framed, but had been hung on the wall with pushpins. She got up and walked over to take a closer look. As she studied the pictures, she wondered if she would be—she stopped. She was lucky. She saw a picture of Marine in her fire uniform. Standing with her was a man she didn't recognize. But, the lady standing to the right of Marine, she would know anywhere. It was her old friend from their INR days—Betsy.

Aunt Jeannie turned and scanned the room to see if anyone was watching her. No one was. She walked up close to Marine's picture and pulled it down off the wall, stashing it quickly into her blouse. She then walked on around the room looking at more pictures.

"Ma'am!" Belle called to Aunt Jeannie. She turned around. "Ma'am, your lunch is ready."

"Thank you." Aunt Jeannie walked over to her table, sat down, and began to enjoy her meal. She had not eaten since early morning. She was hungry.

FOUR

SHERMAN RETURNS

Fire Chief Edwin Altizer came stomping into the Muster Room, a meeting place for the fire investigators. All heads turned to his booming voice, "Letsco! Why aren't you in my office now? I don't have all day!" He turned, marched into his office, slamming the door as he began to pull the blinds over the glass windows.

"You've done it now!" Tom began to chide Marine.

"Lay off. You don't know that he's mad at me. It could be something else."

"Seriously? You seriously believe that? You better take your coat with you. The way he sounded you just may be heading out the door," Matt chimed in.

Marine walked over to his office door, waved back at the guys, and prayed she still had a job.

"What took you so long?" Chief Altizer said as he slammed some papers into a file. "No need to answer. Take a seat. And, don't worry. You're not fired. Yet!"

She took a deep breath, adjusted the chair, and waited. Chief Altizer continued shuffling papers around his desk.

"You know, Letsco. I think I've been on this job too long. I'm not in this dress uniform just to look pretty. I just came from up on the hill. The top brass just ripped me a new one over these arson fires. Even the Mayor is getting involved. Thank God, it's Friday. What a cluster this is turning into. I'm sure you have news that is going to put me into a cheerier mood."

"We've had nine fires in the last week that we can confirm are related and have the signature of the arsonist that Fire Marshal Willard and I briefed you about last Friday. Since then, there have been three fire investigations that we suspect are related."

"What? Suspect? Why?"

"Chief, the fire scenes are being shermanized."

"By who?"

"Captain Bottoms' station."

"Captain Bottoms?"

"Yes."

Chief Altizer got up and walked over to a window that offered a view of the city. He turned back around, "You don't think that he's—" Chief Altizer broke off mid-sentence.

"It's hard to say at this point. Tom and I are not rejecting anyone as a potential suspect."

"Good. Keep after it. And, Letsco, one other thing. I'm forming a Special Investigative Unit that the Brass has decided we need to focus on this arsonist since he or she is covering a lot of territory. You heard about the three fatalities over in Salem?"

"Yes, sir." Marine bowed her head. "I didn't know the victims, but it was a husband, wife, and their six-year old child. The media is covering the fire with extra sensationalism. Who will be the lead of the unit?"

"Battalion Chief Wayne Foglesong. Do you know him?" Marine tried to hide her smile.

"Yes, sir. He was my captain at Chestnut Mountain."

"Good. He'll know your work ethic and will use your skills," Chief Altizer motioned that she could go. Marine got up to leave. "Letsco."

"Yes, sir?"

"Fill Willard and the other investigators in on what you all will be doing. And, I want you to serve as lead when Foglesong is not here."

"Yes, sir."

Marine closed the door and walked past her desk and on around to the processing lab. In the lab, she walked over to the big touch screen that hung on the wall, swiped her hand over it to wake it up, and began looking at the notes they had gathered. She pulled up some maps and diagrams of different scenes. There was something about the fire scenes that kept nagging at her, but she couldn't put her finger on it. At least, not yet.

"What're you doing?" Tom walked into the room.

"I'm trying to figure out why Captain Bottoms would have his men shermanize the fire scenes. And, it's hard to prove, since he's salvaging, overhauling, and cleaning out the fire to prevent rekindle. He's overly aggressive in his process. That aggressive approach is destroying a lot of evidence, which I think he wants to do. Just like Sherman did when he tore through Atlanta."

"Are you sure?" Tom walked over to one of the boxes from the most recent fire. "What makes you think there just isn't any evidence to find?"

"We've had nine fires in the last two weeks that we've managed to confirm were done by the same arsonist. Then, we get these next three fires in the Chestnut Mountain district, and all three of them, at first, look like they will fit the pattern. Yet, we can't find the puzzle pieces. We can't find any other related clues we've been documenting. What do you think?"

"I think that maybe we need to talk with the firefighters at Station Three."

"Let's plan to go visit them tomorrow."

"I'm not sure you should go, Marine. How about let's send Charles and Matt? That way, Captain Bottoms won't get too suspicious if he is really sabotaging the works on purpose."

"I like that idea."

"What did the Chief say?"

"That's another thing. Let's go talk with Matt and Charles."

* * * * *

Fire Marshal Charles Massie drove to the Chestnut Mountain Station Three early Saturday evening where he and Matt Pike would conduct their interviews.

"Matt," Charles said as he swung the car into the parking lot of Station Three. "I've been meaning to ask you. What happened to you the other night? The gang was together. Marine said you told her you'd be coming, but you never showed."

Matt turned and looked at Charles. "What? I never told Marine I'd be there. Where did she get that idea from? I never came in the office."

"I don't know, man. I'm just saying. You missed a good time, though." They walked into Station Three around six Saturday evening to interview the members of C Shift.

"This used to be my old station," Charles said as he rapped his hand on the kitchen door facing. "Hello? Anyone in here?"

"Charles! Come on in and pop a squat," firefighter George "Fish" Fisher said. He got up and shook Charles' hand. "How are you, man? I haven't seen you in years."

"Not doing badly. Let me introduce you to Matt Pike. He's another FM working with me. Where is everybody?"

A Time for Fire

"Glad to meet you, Matt. Hey, did I see you at the Boiler Room Lounge the other night? You were enjoying yourself." Fish said as he extended a hand to Matt.

Matt shook his hand, "Not me. It must have been a twin." Charles and Fish laughed. Matt frowned as he wondered what was going on. It couldn't have been Pat. Matt didn't want to tell the truth about his twin brother. What would everyone think of him if he shared he had a psychopathic brother that loved to set fires? It wouldn't look good on his career. So, he kept it quiet. Besides, he was on lock ward at the hospital for the criminally insane three counties over. They would have told me if he escaped. But, he couldn't have escaped, could he? Matt wondered.

Fish continued talking, "There's five of us on this week. We've had a couple people get injured, Lt. Ron James and Dennis Ray. You probably knew him as 'Willie.' Roy should be around back working on a hose that was crimped. I'm serving as the acting lieutenant while Ron is out. And, you know, when Letsco got promoted they never replaced her position. Doc White, you remember him, don't you?" Charles shook his head. "He's about ready to retire. We're sure going to miss him, I'll tell you that. And, of course, Crab is still here. He'll never leave."

"Where is your captain?" Matt asked as he took a seat. "You don't mind if I pull up a chair, do you?"

"Captain Bottoms doesn't come in during C Shift. He generally leaves just as we're coming in. Though the last two weeks, he's come out on a couple of our fire calls. He'll be back in at seven, tomorrow morning. Help yourself. I'm just doing some paperwork. Want some coffee? We always have hot coffee." Matt and Charles shook their heads no. "What can I do you for?"

"We'd like to interview you and the rest of C Shift about your last three fires."

"The Captain knows about this?"

"No," Charles said. "Is there a problem?"

"None that I know of. Interview away. The others will be in at different times. Doc and Crab are out checking fire hydrants. It's getting dark, so they should be returning to the station in about twenty minutes or so. Of course, Ron and Willie won't be here, but they haven't been on the last two fire calls, as they were injured on the first one."

"We'll probably visit them at their homes," Matt said. "You know, I believe I will take some of that coffee. It smells good."

"Help yourself to some of those sweets. We snuck them in. I'm trying to cut back. Let me finish this last page, and I'll be ready to answer your questions."

Matt poured himself some coffee and motioned to see if Charles wanted any. Charles shook his head no again. Matt pulled out a sweet roll from under the clear plastic dome that covered a tray filled with sweets. He snapped it back into place making a sound that echoed throughout the kitchen.

"Sorry about the noise," Matt said as he sat back in his seat and bellied up to the table.

"You hungry?" Charles asked with a tone that said he knew the answer.

"I love a fresh sweet roll. There's something about pecans, cinnamon, and bread blended into a luscious swirl." Matt grinned as he opened his mouth wide and took a large bite.

"Okay. I'm ready," Fish said. He got up and placed his paperwork in one of the inboxes sitting at the mail slots against the far wall.

"Don't you have an office where your reports can be stored and protected until your office help comes in to type them?" Charles asked.

"We did when Battalion Chief Foglesong was our captain. Captain Bottoms took that away when he came. He said he was going to set the room aside for something, but he's never done anything with it to my knowledge."

Charles and Matt exchanged glances. Charles began the interview.

"Fish, tell me about the work you and your team have done when cleaning up after a fire has been brought under control and extinguished. What instructions have you received and from whom?"

"As you know from when you were here, and, even when Captain Foglesong, excuse me, Battalion Chief Foglesong was here as captain. We were not too aggressive as we were told we shouldn't disturb too much evidence in case the fire was not accidental." Charles nodded his head.

"Fish, that's how we are all taught," Matt chimed in and popped the last bite of sweet roll into his mouth.

"Yes, well. Captain Bottoms had Lt. James change that process. He said that we needed to make sure that the fire was out. He explained

A Time for Fire

how one time he fought a fire, extinguished it, and left. Then the shift had to report back to a rekindling of the fire. It makes sense. But, it seems to me he may be doing it a little too aggressively."

"Why? What makes you say that?" Matt asked while he took notes.

"You know, it is one of those funny things. You know it, but you can't explain how."

"What's going on in here?" Captain Bottoms walked in. "Who are you men?"

Charles and Matt stood up. Fish remained seated. "This is Fire Marshal Charles Massie. He was with this house a few years ago. And, the other gentleman is Fire Marshal Matt Pike."

Charles extended his hand to shake Captain Bottoms' hand, but Captain Bottoms motioned him to stop.

"There's no need to shake hands. You won't be staying here long. You didn't ask me permission to speak with my men. You can leave and go through proper channels."

"Captain, sir. We do not need permission. We are conducting an active fire investigation." Matt stood up and walked over toward Captain Bottoms. "Besides, Captain. I would think you'd welcome our help in determining who is responsible for the rash of fires we've been having in our region."

Captain Bottoms took a step backwards. "Yes. I am. But, I should know when my people are being investigated."

"Captain. Your people are not being investigated. We are simply asking questions regarding the fire scenes. We will be talking to each member of C Shift, including you. And, we will talk with you in your office. At this point, Matt and I can say without hesitation that no one is being investigated. Besides, why would we consider one of our own to be an arsonist? There is no reason. Now, is there?"

Captain Bottoms walked over toward the kitchen counter. He turned back and smiled. "No. No, there isn't. I'm working hard at making this station the best in the region. I hope you understand. I want my people to be excellent at their work, and I expect to be rewarded accordingly."

Matt looked at Charles. He then looked at Fish, who had his head down. Interesting, he thought. He expects to be rewarded. "Sir, Charles and I will work to do what we can to help you receive the reward you deserve. Now, we'd like to get back to our investigation, if that is okay?"

"Sure." Captain Bottoms continued to stand and stir his coffee.

"Sir, we do have the right to interview each person alone. Sergeant Fisher was just finishing up his report when you came in. May we finish our time with him alone?"

"Sure." Captain Bottoms walked out and shut the door to the kitchen. He opened it back up. "You know. You could use my office if you wish. It will give you more privacy." He closed the door, again.

"I think we'd do better in here if you want to know my thinking about it," Fish said as he got up and walked over to the sink. "Now, where were we?"

* * * * *

Captain Bottoms walked into his office and slammed his cup down. Coffee lapped up over the edges in two directions covering the papers lying on the desk with a dark brown liquid. He walked over to his wall of framed samurai soldiers. He moved the center one that was an ink drawing of a samurai flashing a happy grin with his sword held high. His costume was bright yellow with shades of red, pink, and burgundy woven with vines and leaves. It gave the feeling of being gay and happy.

The Captain replaced the happy samurai with one that gave the impression of despair. The samurai's head was down as well as his sword. His costume was a dull grey with shades of black woven with leather and metal ornaments. It depicted gloom and doom. The third picture was clearly one of murder and revenge coupled with hatred. The samurai's face distorted with outrage and anger, stood in a fighting stance; his sword raised ready to remove an enemy's head from its shoulders with one swift move. The samurai costume of the third looked as though it had been covered in blood and gore. It portrayed evil.

He spoke to the last picture. "I'm not ready for you yet. But, I'm moving in that direction. If I've made myself a target, so be it. They'll have to prove I shermanized Letsco's investigations. Poor thing. Life has gotten hard for her. They'll never get enough evidence. I'll just have to raise the stakes a little and see what happens." Bottoms moved the samurai of despair to the center position. He picked up his hat, walked out his office door letting it close behind him.

A Time for Fire

* * * * *

Marine was standing by her desk, gathering a few papers. She and Tom had spent the better part of the evening documenting the last arson fires. She was tired. She looked at the clock. It was close to ten.

"Letsco!" Charles called to her as he and Matt walked into the office area. "You're still here. Good."

"You guys are just now getting back? I thought I'd missed you."

"Yep. We have some interesting pieces of information." Matt walked over to his desk, took off his coat, and sat down. "Interviewing people is a lot of work. I'd rather mull around a fire scene any day." Marine smiled at him.

"So, what did you find out?"

"We believe that Captain Bottoms has a hard-on for you. He's definitely shermanizing the fire scenes. Every one of the shift that we spoke with said he instructed them to be more aggressive with their cleanup and salvage work. And, Fish said he felt like the man was crazy."

"Trust me, I know he is." Marine sat down in her chair. "Well, did any of them happen to give you anything we can use as evidence?"

"Fish said that he saw two puzzle pieces at the last two fires, but Captain Bottoms told him to clean up good. He didn't know what happened to them."

"That doesn't surprise me. Captain Bottoms wants to make sure I have a hard time solving this one. We'll give him time. He'll make a mistake we can use against him. I'm beginning to think he could be our arsonist. Whoever is doing it knows and understands firefighters and how we work a fire. Maybe he has been a firefighter before? Or, heaven forbid still is. Captain Bottoms shermanizing the fire scenes don't make him the arsonist, yet. But, it does make it easy to suspect him for it."

"Have you seen those samurai pictures in his office?" Charles asked as he handed Marine the notes from their interviews.

"Yes. Captain Bottoms made a point of explaining how he uses those pictures. Did Fish tell you the story?"

"Yes. You look at the one in the middle and that's the mood he is in. Well, when we left today, he was already gone as we walked by his office. The middle picture was the one Fish said he calls 'despair.' I guess he got nervous about us being there," Charles chuckled.

"He should. He's a crazy man. I wouldn't want to be alone with him at a fire that's for sure," Matt said. "It's late. I'm hungry. I'm going home."

"Hungry? What? You've eaten all day. How many sweet rolls did you eat?"

"Oh, I don't know. I'm a growing boy. Leave me alone."

"You'll grow to be as big as a horse if you're not careful," Charles said as he reached for his hat. "I'm leaving, too. Wait and I'll walk out with you. We good, Marine?"

"Yes. Thanks, guys. I appreciate your hard work today. See you tomorrow!"

* * * * *

Dr. Chester "Chet" Henegar carried the last of the groceries into Aunt Betsy's kitchen. She wasn't his real aunt, but he thought of her in that way. She had saved his life when he didn't know he needed saving. He had come to understand what having family was all about, since he was an orphan, too. Marine had no idea, and he hadn't planned to tell her. But, yesterday, Aunt Betsy had whispered in his ear that he might need to explain to Marine about his life. He had told Marine a little of his story, but he had left out his early history. He hadn't told anyone except Aunt Betsy. That was six years ago when she took him in. He was on his last dime, contemplating suicide. He would have gone through with it if she hadn't intervened. Aunt Betsy walked into the kitchen interrupting his train of thought.

"Oh, Chet. I see you found some fresh Bing cherries. I just love those. I'll make us a nice cherry pie."

"That is why I got them. Besides loving to eat them straight out of the bag, I love a good old homemade cherry pie. When is Marine arriving? It is almost eleven. Has she been getting in late every night?"

"Yes. Just about every night. Ever since she was put on that blasted fire investigative special unit. I don't know why they had to do that."

"Well, it does give her a chance to see Wayne."

"Wayne? How?"

"She has not told you? Wayne is the lead of the unit."

"Oh, my. It all makes sense now, doesn't it? She wants to make an impression. She is so infatuated with him. He is such a handsome man." Aunt Betsy moved the bag of cherries into the refrigerator. "It's too late to make a pie tonight. I'll do that first thing—" A car door slammed. "Oh, I think she's home. Finally! Now, Chet. Remember, you need to talk with her."

"Now? Tonight? Could it wait? I mean, she will be so tired."

"No. You tell her tonight!"

The back porch screened door opened. "Tell me what?"

FIVE

LET'S BE STILL

Marine walked from her cottage at the back of Aunt Betsy's home, Trout House Falls, and up the steps into the kitchen. She looked around and couldn't see anyone, but she could smell the aroma of fresh cinnamon rolls baking in the oven. There was a pot of coffee sitting in the coffee maker. She walked over to it, hoping it was fresh. There wasn't a light, so she touched the side. It was warm, but not hot. She took down a mug and poured some coffee.

"Stop!" Aunt Betsy called as she walked into the kitchen. "That coffee was made yesterday. I haven't made any fresh yet. I'm running behind."

"Oh. Okay," Marine said, pouring the brown liquid down the drain. "It felt warm. When will the rolls come out? I'm starving." Marine put a fresh pot of coffee to brew.

"It's probably where the sun rays hit the pot this morning. As for your rolls, hold your horses, little lady. They'll be another ten or so minutes. Besides, you should eat a more hearty breakfast than just a cinnamon roll. I'll make you eggs and bacon. You can plan to take the cinnamon roll with you when you go into work. I understand Matt loves them."

"Yes, he does. It's a nice idea, but I won't be heading into work today."

"Oh. Why not?"

"I've worked too much and it's a forced day off. I guess I could use it. I am tired. Well, I'm not as tired as I was last night."

"What are you planning to do today?" Aunt Betsy moved the last of the bacon that had been sizzling out of the skillet onto a paper towel to drain. She began beating a couple of eggs. "Do you want toast with your meal?"

"No. I think I'll eat the cinnamon roll as my bread. Man. That bacon smells heavenly. As for what I'm doing today, I think Wayne and I are going to go into town and maybe explore. I'd love to go to Belle's, have lunch, and maybe go for a ride to the dam or Graham's Park. I don't know. I'd love to just enjoy the outdoors. All I've seen the past few weeks is darkness, gloom, and fire. And all I've smelt is smoke, soot, and burnt things. I'm looking forward to some sunshine and fresh air."

"I bet you are," Chet said as he walked in the back door. "Happy July morning, Aunt Betsy."

"Good morning, Chet. Sit down there and I'll fix your breakfast next. You are staying to eat, aren't you?"

"I had not planned on it until I smelled those cinnamon rolls and bacon all the way down the driveway. You sure know how to attract someone to your kitchen."

"You going into town to your office?" Marine asked as she took her plate from Aunt Betsy. "How much longer on those rolls?"

Aunt Betsy opened the oven door and pulled out a large pan. Steam bellowed up and around the room chasing their noses. "I'll set these here and cover them. They need to cool just a bit. Then, I'm going to ice them. So, you won't be able to eat them for another five minutes or so."

"Really, now, Aunt Betsy. Five more minutes? I'll have my eggs eaten by then."

"What? You slow down and you will have plenty of eggs and bacon to eat with your roll when it's ready." Aunt Betsy moved back to the stove. "Chet?"

"Yes, ma'am?"

"How do you want your eggs?"

"Sunny side up is fine or even scrambled. I'm with Marine. I would just as soon eat the cinnamon rolls."

"No, you will have a good breakfast, too. I declare I don't know what's gotten into you, young people. I have to make you eat good food." Marine and Chet giggled.

Marine watched Chet get up and fix himself some coffee. "You need any, Marine?"

"No, I'm fine. Thanks."

"Will you have time today for you and me to meet for a bit? I would like to talk with you about a few things."

"Well, I don't know. Is it about what you mentioned last night as I came in and you said we'd talk later?"

"Yes."

"Thanks for letting me sleep first. I was so tired, I'm not sure I would have stayed awake. Anyway, to answer your question, Wayne and I are meeting around eleven. Can you meet before then?"

"I think I could. Could you come by my office?"

"You can meet with Marine in there in the parlor. I don't mind," Aunt Betsy said as she placed Chet's plate on the table. "Your plate is ready. Don't let your food get cold."

Chet moved back to his seat.

"Are the rolls ready now?" Marine asked as she reached up under the cloth that was covering them. Aunt Betsy smacked her hand with a spoon. "Ouch! What did you do that for?"

"I haven't iced them yet. Now, you wait."

"Yes, ma'am."

"Let's meet in the parlor, Chet. It's okay with me if it is with you. It will save us time and I'll be able to meet with you for sure, then."

Chet looked over at Aunt Betsy. He looked back at Marine. "Okay. We can plan to talk right after you and I have a cinnamon roll."

"I have an idea, Chet. You both can take your rolls with your coffee into the parlor and enjoy them while you talk."

"You are going to let us eat in the parlor?"

"Don't sound so shocked, Chet. We've eaten in there before."

"Not since the preacher was here."

"Well, it's time we change it up a bit, then." They all laughed.

* * * * *

After Aunt Betsy helped Chet and Marine carry their food and beverages to the parlor, she said, "I'll leave you two to talk. Know that I love you both."

Marine looked after Aunt Betsy and when she was safely out of earshot, Marine said, "What was that about?"

"I am not sure, but I think she hopes you will not be alarmed by what I am about to share with you. Before I do, I want to ask you how you are doing with your new job and your new life here in New Brook? Are you doing okay with what you learned happened with Ana-Geliza and Aunt Betsy?"

"Well, Chet, I must say, you've asked a lot there for me to cover. First, as you saw last night, I'm working hard—harder than I ever worked as an assassin, I can tell you that. Course, I do not have to struggle with staying alive. But, my job as a fire investigator is very interesting. I get to use a lot of the skills I acquired while I was an assassin."

"Interesting. Such as?"

"My detective skills as well as my ability to be unseen. I've used those to good advantage on several occasions when I wanted to check out a crowd that has gathered at a suspected arson fire. Once, it helped me nab a guy who had set a fire so he could get even with his girlfriend. What else did you ask me?"

"Your new life here. How is it going? Evidently, not bad since you are seeing Wayne, I take it."

"You're right. I struggled with that for a while. I thought I was in love with Drake. But, I think that was just me feeling desperate to get away from TRANS. Don't get me wrong. Drake is a wonderful person, not to mention not too bad looking. But, I think Wayne might be a better pick for me. So, I'm getting to know him. I never really knew Drake. I would have liked to get to know him better, but I didn't. As for my living arrangements, I like living in the back cottage. I think I'll maintain that for a while. Then, who knows?"

Chet leaned forward, took a bite of a cinnamon roll, and drank some coffee. "And the events with Ana-Geliza?"

"I was hoping you'd overlook that one. I'm fine with it. I wish I knew if she were really dead. I mean, she did rise out of the ashes like a phoenix twice before. They do say three is the charm or is it nine if you're a cat? Anyway, I am at peace with Aunt Betsy killing her. She had to do what she had to do. I believe she is dead. We haven't heard from her again. She made it clear she hated me enough to come back from the dead. Let's hope she doesn't do that." Marine tilted her head and grinned.

Chet chuckled. "Yes. Yes, I can see why you would hope that would not happen. I am glad you are not having any second thoughts regarding your choices. You did have to go after Ana-Geliza in order to save Aunt Betsy. As a result, you ended up saving yourself. I hope that when I finish sharing my story, you will continue to think highly of me."

Marine leaned forward, took a bite of a cinnamon roll, and looked up stunned at Chet's comment. "Your story? I thought we were in here to talk about me like we always do. Besides, don't you love those cinnamon rolls!"

"Yes. They are delish. And no, I need to share with you the truth about my past and who I am."

"Wait a minute. Don't tell me you were an agent too for some diabolical, espionage organization and you've been waiting on your chance to take me out." They laughed together.

"No. No. Nothing like that. You see, Aunt Betsy is not my real aunt. As a matter of fact, until six years ago, I had no idea she even existed. I was at a very low point in my life. I told you about the two patients who killed themselves. Well, I tried to do the same." Marine set her plate down and placed her elbows on her knees. She looked intently at Chet. "I was almost successful. Aunt Betsy stepped in and saved my life."

"Chet. I had no idea."

"I know. I had not planned to tell you this, but for some reason, Aunt Betsy thinks it best that you know. I really want you to understand how wonderful she has been to me. She has helped me rebuild my life, my practice, and to give me the confidence I needed to be whole again. The cruise, it was only my second time away from her."

"No. You wouldn't have known it. Hell, I'm supposed to pick up on things like that. I never even guessed. Course, for the majority of the time I knew you, I didn't know who I was. So, I guess that works."

"Marine, Aunt Betsy has been the support I have needed to become me again. If she had died under Ana-Geliza's hand, I am not sure what I would have done. I am so grateful to you for being here, for saving her, and for being my friend. You have got to promise me one thing." Chet paused briefly and went on, "You will try your best to trust Aunt Betsy no matter what you learn about her and her life." Chet felt he was going to break down. But, he held it back. "I am trying not to cry, but I want you to know that no matter what, I will always consider you and Aunt Betsy as my family. You are the first patient that I can state with certainty I helped since my last crisis. You are very important to me."

"I'm touched, Chet. This is very important to know. I'm glad Aunt Betsy insisted you tell me. And, I'll do my best to understand what you mean about trusting Aunt Betsy."

"Hello? Anyone here?" Wayne said as he came into the parlor. "I knocked, but no one answered. I hope you don't mind me barging on in."

Marine got up and walked over to Wayne. She kissed him on the cheek. "No. This is great, but you are a little early, aren't you?"

"Yes. I have a surprise and I couldn't wait. Are you ready to go? You guys looked so serious when I came in."

Marine looked at Chet. "Chet, can we talk more later?"

"Sure. You both go have a wonderful time. I am glad we got to talk. I will let Aunt Betsy know how it all went."

"Great, Chet. I'll see you later. Wayne, come with me out to the cottage, I'll need to get my bag. Oh, Chet, tell Aunt Betsy I'll catch up with her later." Marine and Wayne went out of the parlor.

"Is she gone?" Aunt Betsy said as she walked into the parlor from the kitchen.

"Have you been listening?"

"Yes."

"Aunt Betsy. You might as well have been sitting right here."

"This way, I could hear her reaction without wondering if she was covering up her true feelings."

"Sometimes, I truly do not understand who you really are."

Aunt Betsy walked over to Chet and put her arms around him. "You know enough for now."

SIX

....

BRANDY SHAKE WOMAN

Wayne and Marine walked out to his car, a sleek BMW Three series in navy blue. She watched as he opened the door for her. He then walked around and got in on the driver's side.

"You know, Wayne, it doesn't matter how many times I ride in your car, it always seems like it is new. How do you keep it looking so nice?"

"I wash it." Wayne winked. "Now, you haven't asked where we are going."

"Nope."

"Well, first, we're heading to The Hardware Company for lunch."

"The Hardware Company. Where is it located?"

"Hillsville."

"Hillsville? Where is that?"

"Oh, you've not been there. Good. Up the road apiece. We'll go up the Blue Ridge Parkway—"

"No way!" Marine sat up, turned, and looked at Wayne. "You're kidding me right?"

"No. Why?"

"When Chet and I first arrived, I got to learn about and use his console that had access to the Internet. Out of curiosity, I decided I'd learn what I could about New Brook and the surrounding area. The first place I read about was the Blue Ridge Parkway. I can't believe it. I've lived here almost two years and this will be my first time going there. What's it like?"

Wayne laughed. "Hold on. We'll only be on it for a little ways. Besides, the best time to see it is in the fall of the year when the leaves are turning. We'll need to make plans to come back this fall. You should be able to see some pretty scenery even though it is early in July. I'm glad we have air conditioning. It's going to be a scorcher out there today."

"Oh, this is so exciting. Can we pull off and look at the different views along the way?"

"Yes. We'll have time to look at a couple. But, I do have some other things for us to do besides riding the Parkway and eating, you know."

Marine smiled and sat back. "You will tell me when we get on the Parkway, right?"

"Hahaha. Marine, you are so cute when you're excited. There will be a sign. Besides, the road is different from regular secondary roads. We can only go forty-five miles per hour. It will take us about an hour to get to Hillsville from here."

"An hour? Oh, I had no idea. Well, you better get to it then."

* * * * *

"We're turning onto the Parkway now. See the brown sign?"

"Can we stop and let me take a picture?"

After stopping along the way another six times, taking pictures, and letting Marine take in a couple of views, they drove past Mabry Mill.

"Hey!" Wayne pulled over at the sound of Marine's scream. "Why'd you go by that mill so fast? We've got to stop there."

"If we stop there now, we'll never make Hillsville. What do you want to do?"

"Let's stop here. It has a restaurant. I'd just as soon eat here. We can go to Hillsville another day."

"Okay. I'm at your service."

Marine chuckled to herself. The last time she heard someone say that to her was when Bajatand, her waiter on the Stellar Cruise ship would serve her. She wondered where he was and what he was doing.

Wayne pulled his car into a parking space. Marine jumped out, ran over to the water's edge, and then began taking several pictures of the mill and pond. It was working that day, grinding flour. There were several tents setup near the back area of the mill. She ran ahead and motioned for Wayne to follow her. When he caught up to her, she was watching a blacksmith hammer a horseshoe.

"I was beginning to think you weren't going to come over."

"I was beginning to think you hadn't figured out you had left me in your dust." Wayne put his arm around her and kissed her cheek. "Are you having fun?"

"Yes. This is so interesting."

"Are you going to eat anything?"

"Oh, sure. We have time, don't we?"

Wayne looked at his watch. "It is already eleven o'clock. We need to be back in town at least by two, or we won't get to do all I have planned."

Marine turned to him. "What do you have planned anyway that we have to be on a schedule?"

"Something fun. Now, I'm starving. Come on. We can come back for another visit." Marine walked away reluctantly.

Inside the Mabry Mill Restaurant, they were seated near the far wall. They could look out over the back property and hear the water flowing from the millrace.

"This is lovely. I have always wanted a back porch like this, screened in, and a table or two to enjoy a meal. Oh, we'd need a nice wood stove or fireplace, and a place to take a nap, like a hammock or day bed."

Wayne smiled. "You've got it all figured out?"

"Yes, sir. I know what I want, where I want it, and how I want to live from now on. None of this dangerous stuff for me. No siree!"

"Have you decided what you want to eat? You can still have breakfast or you can enjoy a nice lunch?"

"You said it was almost eleven before. Hmmm. I think I'll have lunch. Aunt Betsy fixed a wonderful breakfast this morning. What are you going to have?"

"I love their country ham sandwich. I think I'll have that with some gelatin salad and unsweetened iced tea."

"That sounds lovely. I'll have the same."

A young waitress walked up. "Howdy, folks. Do you know what you'll be having?"

Wayne placed the order for both of them. Marine got up and decided she'd walk around and see what was for sale in the gift store. While looking at the different gifts, she went into the women's bathroom. Standing there was a woman that she thought she might recognize. The lady lowered the brim of her summer hat down over her face, threw her paper towel in the trash can, and left.

Marine stood there for a moment. "No, it couldn't be," she said aloud.

"Couldn't be what, Dearie?" A stranger said.

"Oh, nothing. Guess I was talking out loud for no reason." Marine left the bathroom, but the feeling she should have known the woman wouldn't leave her.

"Are you okay?" Wayne asked as Marine took her seat.

"Yes. Yes, I think so."

"Well, you don't look like it. You look like you saw a ghost."

"Nope. I don't think I saw a ghost. I do think I saw someone that I should know."

* * * * *

Wayne pulled onto Tazewell Street, off Main, and about a block up from Belle's restaurant.

"Where are we headed now?" Marine said as they drove by Petal's floral shop. "Doesn't it look nice?"

"I'm taking you to see something I think you will love. What looks nice?"

"Petal's new store window. I just love how she fixes her flowers. Course, I love Kelly's Kreations, too. Don't you?"

"I've not thought much about either one lately. Guess I should remember those two places in the future. By the way, when is your birthday?" Wayne parked the car in front of Peggy's Place across the street from Petal's.

"January 15. Why?" Marine got out of the car. "And, where are we going?"

"Follow me. I'll make a note of your birthday. I think I missed this year's, which won't happen again." He smiled and took Marine by the hand. "Come on. We don't have a lot of time. I told them we'd drop by around one. We're an hour late. We've got to be somewhere else after this stop."

They walked through the initial foyer door and turned right into Peggy's Place.

"Wayne, I don't need my hair done. Peggy has me scheduled in a few weeks."

"Don't be silly. We're coming here for you to see something."

Peggy yelled out to them as Wayne closed the door to her shop. "I'm finishing up with a customer. I'll be right with you."

"Take your time, Peggy. We're late. No need to make you rush."

Wayne and Marine sat down in the bay window seats. There was a little chirping noise. "Do you hear that?"

"What?" Wayne smiled.

"It almost sounds like puppies."

"That's because it is," Peggy said coming into her waiting area while drying her hands. My client will be under the hair dryer for about thirty minutes. You timed dropping by perfectly." Peggy reached down and pulled up a box. Inside were three little puppies.

"Oh, my," Marine said. "May I hold one?"

"Sure." Peggy moved the box closer. "Pick them all up if you want. They love to roll around and walk on the floor."

"How old?"

"They are four weeks old. We're looking for homes. Do you know of any?"

"I don't know. What kind?"

"They are a cross between a Brittany Spaniel and a Cocker. Don't you just love their faces?"

"You have two males and one female."

"Yes, and they are free to a good home."

Wayne looked at Marine and handed her the male he was holding. "He is so loving, Marine. Don't you think you should get him?"

"Wayne? What makes you think I could own a dog? I don't even own my own place."

"I've already talked it over with Aunt Betsy. She is fine with you having him in the cottage. Besides, she has the large farm. He would love running and playing there."

Marine confided in Wayne that she always loved dogs. She shared how she lost her German Shepard, Colombo, when he was young. Tears welled up in her eyes.

"It's okay, Marine. I know how you're feeling. I had a Blue Tick Beagle named Shiloh. He was such a fun dog. We went everywhere together. Every day, he'd get his breakfast, and then he'd go around the neighborhood to get treats from all the neighbors. They all loved him. One day, he went about doing his treat gathering, but he never came home. He was old. We think he went around and said his goodbyes, then went off to die somewhere where he knew he wouldn't be found. It broke my heart." Marine noticed Wayne was wiping his eyes.

"It's amazing how a little animal such as this can sneak right into your heart." Marine looked down at the fudgesicle-colored face splotched with white. The little puppy stretched up and licked her nose. "I don't know, I guess I could. I'll think about it." Marine handed the puppy back to Wayne. She couldn't bear to put him down.

"Peggy? When will they be ready to take home?"

Peggy stepped back into the room. "Oh, in about another four weeks or so."

"Well, which one do you want?"

"This one, of course." Marine picked the little puppy back up.

"Here, I'll tie a little bow around his neck. He's a cutie, isn't he?" Peggy said.

"What will you name him?" Wayne asked as he got up off the floor.

"I'm not sure. I'll think about that, too. When do you need to know, Peggy?"

"I'd like to know today. I do have some other people coming by."

"Oh. Well. Gees, Wayne. What should I do? He is so cute." Marine looked down at him and he licked her face again. "Okay. I'll take him." She turned to Wayne, "You're sure it's okay with Aunt Betsy?"

"Yes."

Marine handed the puppy back to Peggy. "Let's go. I'm not sure I can leave without him now."

"Thanks, Peggy."

"No problem guys. See you later."

"Yes, see you tonight." Wayne closed the door as they walked out to his car.

"Where are we going that we'll be seeing her tonight?"

"That's my next surprise."

"You sure are full of them."

"Call me lucky Pierre."

Marine busted out laughing as they got back in Wayne's car. He pulled out onto Monroe Street and turned right.

"What do you think about heading to the lake?"

"Oh, my. I love the lake. Are we going back to your little piece of land?"

"Yes. I want your opinion on something."

After about thirty minutes, Wayne pulled his car to a stop. The water of the lake shimmered in the late afternoon sun.

"It's so beautiful here."

"Yes, Marine, it is." Wayne reached over and touched Marine's face. She wasn't sure what she wanted, but she knew she wanted him.

They kissed.

* * * * *

"We probably should go back to the car and head over to Connie and Martin Thomas' boat. We're meeting them, and Peggy and Jerry to have a light dinner, some drinks, and play cards."

"After the lazy afternoon we've had, do I look okay? I don't look too wrinkled, do I?"

"Heavens, no. You look lovely."

A Time for Fire

They arrived at the Thomas' sailboat about six. A light breeze blew across the water. Marine smiled and thought about the afternoon they had spent together.

"This is turning into a fabulous day off. I'm so glad you planned my day. I've never had anyone do that for me before." Wayne parked the car, got out, and walked around to open her car door. "And, it's been a while since a man has acted like a gentleman, too."

"It is my pleasure."

"I feel funny coming here and not bringing something."

"Oh, don't you worry. I have something right back here." Wayne walked back to the trunk; it opened automatically when he pushed a button. He lifted out a gift bag. "I always come prepared when I go to the lake."

"Evidently, you do. I never dreamed you'd find such a nice place for us to lounge earlier under that tree on your lake property. You had a blanket, pillows, and wine with cheese in a cooler stashed inside that tree." They began to walk toward the boat. "When did you plan all this? I didn't even know I was going to be able to take today off until two days ago."

"I have my sources." Wayne winked at Marine. She felt special, but also a little cautious. Was she dropping Drake too soon? Should Wayne be her interest now? Just because Drake was gone didn't mean she should forget him so easily. He did save her life on more than one occasion. Her thoughts were interrupted.

"There you guys are," Connie beamed as they walked up to the side of the boat. "Come on aboard. We're so looking forward to being with you guys. Peggy and Jerry are already here. Martin is down inside fixing drinks. Do you have a preference?"

"I'd love a Brandy Shake," Marine said as she stepped over into the boat.

"I'll take whatever beer you have."

"Martin thought you might want some of his Jack Daniels. Will that work? I think he's already got it fixed."

"Sure. I'll never turn that down."

They greeted Peggy and Jerry, and then settled into eating some lovely snacks and hors-d'oeuvres that Connie had prepared. It wasn't long after that they began to play cards.

"That's the third hand I've lost in a row. Dang. What's the matter with me?" Jerry said as he stood up. "Anyone need a refill? I'm going down to visit the john and refresh my drink."

"I'll go with you," Wayne said. "I need to do both, too."

"Well, I might as well join you guys," Martin said.

The men went down into the lower section of the boat leaving the girls a chance to talk.

"Now, tell me, are you really taking that precious little puppy?" Connie asked Marine. "Peggy filled me in when she got here."

"You looked so suited to that little thing. Wayne just knew you'd fall in love with it. He said so when he asked if I'd bring the puppies to the salon and show them to you." Peggy took a slow sip of her drink.

"Really, I had no idea." Marine began to realize that Wayne had manipulated the entire day. She wasn't sure she liked that, or if what she really liked was that he did it and she liked being pampered.

* * * * *

Off the side of the dock near where the Thomas' sailboat was moored, a dark figure in a black wetsuit lowered a backpack into the water. Swimming up next to the craft, the figure was careful to prevent the water from lapping up against its sides. Next, removing a knife, the backpack was secured up against the hull. After about ten minutes, the dark figure swam past two docks, emerged out of the water, and sat on the edge of the decking.

A low voice said, "The plan is set?"

"Yes. Just as you directed."

"Good. Here's your money. Now, here's my bonus."

The dark figure slumped over, blood gushed from the neck area, and the limp body slipped back into the water not making a sound.

SEVEN

....

MORE THAN ONE ENEMY

Pat had bought every newspaper printed in the region. He held six in his hands. Some were small and thin, while one was thick with lots of those stupid insert ads. He'd dropped a pile of them on the fire. He hoped it would burn a long time. He would continue feeding it with the sticks he'd gathered in the back. Dave's house was all his now. He could hang out wherever he wanted. There was no one left to tell anyone his true identity, except for Jack Manytoes, who was now safely locked up and no one would believe any story he told. Not after Pat made sure his letter implicated Jack in helping Pat escape. And, then of course, dear brother, Matt. Pat chuckled to himself.

He picked up Dave's cell phone and dialed Matt's office.

"Evansham Fire Investigations and Bomb Squad Team. How may I help you?" the lady on the other end of the line said.

"This is Damon Gregory. I'm with the Evansham News Media. I was supposed to meet Matt. I missed my appointment due to a wreck. Can you look on your GPS system and tell me where he is right now that I might catch up with him?"

"Oh, well. Give me a second and I'll check." Pat could hear keys clicking on a computer. "Sir, Matt is out on the north end of the county investigating a fire. He should be back around seven or seven thirty. Would you like for me to take a message?"

"No, that's fine. I'll touch base with him." Pat hung up the phone. Perfect, he thought. He's at that fire I started two nights ago, Pat thought. A perfect location to snap him up. He looked at his watch. It was five thirty. He could get to Matt before he left the scene. He gathered up his equipment and the tools he would need.

"It won't be long now, brother. Not long at all."

EIGHT

....

YELLOW FLAME BEATS

Fire Marshal Matt Pike drove to the scene of a recent arson fire that had happened a couple of days earlier at an old abandoned farm about twenty miles from town. As he turned down the road that led to the scene, he felt he'd seen the location before, but he couldn't place it. The trailer off to the right was old. A barn had weathered boards that looked like they had stood a long time. The outbuilding beside the barn had been the target and now lay in a pile of rubble. Matt walked the scene, documenting his findings by taking pictures and gathering evidence. He had been working the scene about an hour and half when he found what he hoped he wouldn't—another puzzle piece.

"Damn. This is the work of our arsonist." He reached in his pocket and retrieved his cell. "Seven thirty. I better at least try to tell Letsco what I found. This makes puzzle piece thirty." He looked at his reception. It was good, but his battery was low. Letsco's cell rang and rang, and then went to voice mail.

"Letsco. Sorry to bother you. This is Matt. My cell battery is low, so I'll make this quick. I'm at the fire scene, north end of the county. The farm outbuilding fire. I've found another puzzle piece. It was attached to a piece of paper. I'm telling you this 'cause I won't be in the office tomorrow. I've got to head over to Rockbridge County regarding a family matter. I should be back in the office on Tuesday." Matt fumbled with his phone and dropped the puzzle piece. As he did, it fell upside down. He bent to pick it up and saw the paper had writing on the underside.

"Letsco. You won't believe it. This time the puzzle piece has a message. Give me a second and I'll unfold it so I can read it." Matt's hands were full. He set his camera down on a nearby rock. He opened up the message. The writing was scrolled, a little hard to read, but the message was clear:

Randle the candle has a puzzle for you.
It will be such a scandal when they think it is you!
Oh, my, what will you do?
Randle the candle has got a handle on you.

Matt knew the note was from his brother despite the fact Pat used the stupid name, Randle. Pat always warned him when he was about to frame him for one of his dirty deeds. But, he had just been told that Pat was dead. Or was he? Matt looked around at the area. The familiarity of the scene grew in his mind as he studied the puzzle piece and note.

Pat could have escaped from the hospital, but why would the hospital officials tell him that Pat had died if he didn't? Matt looked closely at the puzzle piece. He knew why the fire scene looked familiar to him. It reminded him of a jigsaw puzzle that he and his twin brother would work as kids. Except for the trailer sitting nearby, the fire scene he was investigating was very similar to the puzzle's picture—an old barn with outbuildings in the background ablaze with yellow and red flames and lots of black and gray smoke. A firefighter stood atop an aerial platform spraying water to extinguish the flames. Matt twirled the puzzle piece in his hand. He looked down and noticed along the edge black letters in fine print that looked like they were written by hand. He read, "It's me."

Matt turned back to his phone.

"Letsco. The—" He dropped his phone as he fell to the ground writhing in pain.

* * * * *

After zapping Matt, Pat managed to blow dust particles of devil's breath in his face. Matt became helpless and had no free will, which enabled Pat to haul his brother to Matt's car without much effort.

Arriving at Dave's house, Pat maneuvered Matt inside where Pat secured him in the same seat he'd used in the kitchen when he tortured Dave. As much fun as he had enjoyed giving pain to Dave, he was going to enjoy torturing Matt even more.

A Time for Fire

Pat was so pleased with himself. He'd managed to snag Matt before his brother had a clue he was anywhere around. And, he now had Matt's vehicle, which meant he'd be able to replace him on the job. No one will be the wiser he thought as he began to take Matt's clothes off.

NINE

....

DIE AND LET LIVE

The driveway was quiet as Wayne and Marine sat in his car, the windows down. The light of a full moon was starting to shine through the tops of the trees that lined the back of Aunt Betsy's property.

"It's a lovely night," Wayne said. "I hope you had a good time today."

"I did. Very relaxing. I enjoyed visiting—" Marine's cell phone began to beep. "Stupid phone. It might be smart, but it's dumb when it comes to timing. Let me see who it is." Marine looked at the screen. "That's odd. I wonder why the phone didn't ring earlier. I have a message from Matt. I'll put it on speaker."

"Should you? How do you know I should hear what he has to say?"

"Relax. He was out on an investigation this evening. He probably found another puzzle piece. You should hear about it anyway since you're the head of the Special Unit." Marine pushed a few keys.

> "Letsco. Sorry to bother you. This is Matt. My cell battery is low, so I'll make this quick. I'm at the fire scene, north end of the county. The farm outbuilding fire. I've found another puzzle piece. It was attached to a piece of paper. I'm telling you this 'cause I won't be in the office tomorrow. I've got to head over to Rockbridge County regarding a family matter. I should be back in the office on Tuesday."

(Rustling sound of something.)

> "Letsco. You won't believe it. This time the puzzle piece has a message. Give me a second and I'll unfold it so I can read it."

(Rustling sound of cell and paper.)

Silence. Marine looked at Wayne. "Has he hung up?"

"No, I don't think so."

> "Letsco. The—"

The phone went dead. "Damn. I wonder what he was going to say."

"You know he found another puzzle piece. He said he wouldn't be in tomorrow. So, I guess we have to wait."

"I don't know. He wouldn't have called unless it was important."

"Marine. Give it a break. You know Matt. He said his phone was about to die. Maybe the battery went dead. Besides, I want to talk about us right now, not work."

Marine placed her cell back in her pocket. "Okay. I'm here. All eyes on you."

"Just the way I like it, too." They embraced.

"Would you like to come in for a night cap?" Wayne smiled.

* * * * *

It was almost eleven thirty when Wayne left the cottage. Marine remembered Aunt Betsy had asked her to come see her when she got home no matter how late. She hooked her cell to the charger and carried both with her as she headed up to see Aunt Betsy.

Opening the screened back door, Aunt Betsy said, "It's about time you let that young man head off to his place. Come on in here. I've got some hot tea made for you along with a cookie or two."

"That young man as you call him is older than I am." Marine walked in and gave Aunt Betsy a quick hug and kiss on the cheek. "I'll just have some tea, if that's okay?"

"Sure. Have a seat and I'll have it right over." Aunt Betsy carried a tray with a teapot, two teacups, some stevia sweetener, and some of her oatmeal raisin cookies. She set the tray down and walked back for two spoons and napkins. "I don't know why, but I always forget these."

"Okay, Aunt Betsy. What gives?" Marine plugged her cell phone charger into an outlet on the counter and made sure it was plugged into the cell phone. She took a seat. "My phone is about to die, so I've got to keep it charged. The arson fires are keeping us all busy these last few weeks."

Aunt Betsy poured the tea and handed a cup to Marine. "What do you mean?"

"About being busy?" Aunt Betsy looked puzzled. "Oh, you mean about when I asked you 'what gives?' It is almost midnight. We're sitting in your kitchen having tea and cookies. What's up?"

"Nothing too serious." She passed the plate of cookies to Marine. "Have one. You'll enjoy it." She smiled as she took one for herself. "But, first tell me about your date."

"It was lovely. We went to Mabry Mill for an early lunch. Then we came back, went by Peggy's Place, and saw some puppies. Have you been in cahoots with Wayne?" Aunt Betsy smiled and shrugged her shoulders. "Well, I don't know if I'm getting one or not. They are precious, though. Have you seen them?"

"Yes. One, a little male. He came running up to me as if he knew me from a prior life."

"There was a little male that acted like he should stay with me now. I almost brought him home. But, they still have to get their shots and to be checked over by a vet. I don't know."

"If you ask me, you are already going to bring one home. It is just a matter of which one."

"You're probably right. You sure you don't mind?"

"No. Besides, we have an entire farm of several acres he can roam without any problems."

"You said, 'he.' I guess we know the one I'll be bringing home." They giggled.

Aunt Betsy refilled her teacup. "Would you like more?" Marine shook her head no. "I guess

I might as well tell you. Can you stay a bit and we talk?"

"Sure. You do know I have to work tomorrow. So, if I'm going to get any sleep, you can talk all you want and I won't interrupt. I promise." Marine smiled and took a cookie. "I might as well enjoy one while we chat."

"It's about my prior life." Marine nodded she understood and waited for Aunt Betsy to continue. "This is harder than I thought it would be." There was a long period of silence. "Marine, I've told you about my early life working at INR, about my friendship with Aunt Jeannie." Marine nodded her head. "Chet shared with you how he is not my real nephew. But, there is more."

"Why does this not surprise me?"

"Please hold your questions."

"Funny. I wish I'd brought paper. I think I'm going to need to make a list." Aunt Betsy got up and retrieved a notepad off her refrigerator with an ink pen. "You're a comedian. Thanks."

"I mentioned before about my work with the Bureau of INR. But, I didn't share how that work cost me my husband and my daughter and her husband as well as their daughter." Aunt Betsy paused.

"No. You didn't mention that part of the story. You lost your entire family? How can you be so calm?"

"I may look calm on the outside, but believe me; I'm scathing on the inside. While at INR, I developed a very close relationship with Aunt Jeannie, as I've told you. We were secret agents together. You know what that means?" Marine looked into Aunt Betsy's eyes. She felt a sudden surge of sorrow for Aunt Betsy. "Yes. I can see in your eyes that you know what that meant. I was an assassin as you were. That's why I didn't hesitate to kill Ana-Geliza." Marine reached out her hand and held Aunt Betsy's. "Your tenderness toward me means more than you will ever know."

"Aunt Betsy, I know the horrors of learning to accept murdering in cold blood. But, I never lost my family because of it. They were already gone. I can't imagine how you must feel. Did you ever learn what caused Aunt Jeannie to turn evil? I know what you said Ana-Geliza had told you, but you had to know she was changing before you talked with Ana-Geliza, didn't you?"

"Sadly, I was so angry over the loss of my husband the year before, and then closely followed by the loss of my daughter and her husband, I didn't pay much attention. We had parted ways when my daughter was killed. Jean was transferred out of INR shortly before their murder. After she transferred out, I only heard snippets of what she was doing. It wasn't obvious to me that she had turned evil. The sad part of it was that I never understood what I heard from my contacts about what was happening to her. I actually didn't believe some of the reports. Twenty years later, I've since come to realize that, in some ways, she was more evil than the people we were hired to commit sabotage and assassinate."

"Oh, my. Aunt Betsy, how long did you continue to work with INR after your daughter's murder?"

"That's another thing. Even though I'm inactive, I still work for them." Marine removed her hand from hers. "Don't be too shocked. As I've told you before, I'm not going to turn you in or give your whereabouts away to anyone. You see, I have a lot of connections and am aware of a lot of things."

Marine sat and pondered what she had heard. She was struggling with the news, but she had to look within herself. "Aunt Betsy, I can't hold this news against you. You took me in when you knew nothing about me. You gave me a roof over my head. You were open to having me here. I must be open to change. I must shed my own flaws and not push them on anyone else. Otherwise, why are we here? If we don't grow and change and become more open-minded to our chosen life, how can we have success?"

Aunt Betsy caressed Marine's hands. "I'm so glad to hear you say this. I was very worried you wouldn't understand. I do want to tell you—" Marine's phone began to ring.

"Sorry. I had better get this. Hello? Wayne?" Marine listened.

"What? No! Oh no!" Marine dropped down to the floor. "How long ago?" She waited.

"Okay. Do we report now?" She looked at Aunt Betsy.

"I understand. Thank you for calling me so soon. I'll be in by seven in the morning." Marine shook her head in disbelief. "Okay. Yes, you try and get some sleep, too." Marine shut off her phone and just stared into space. How in the hell did it happen? She wondered.

"Marine?" Marine felt a gentle hand touch her shoulder.

She looked up. "Oh, Aunt Betsy. I'm so sorry." Marine got up and wrapped her arms around the woman. She led her to the table and they both took a seat.

"Is it Chet?"

"No. But, it is someone close to us. The Thomas' sailboat exploded this evening. They think Connie, Martin, Jerry, and Peggy were aboard. Wayne and I were with them earlier for a light dinner and cards. Oh, Aunt Betsy, this is terrible."

"Was it arson?"

"They don't know yet. The explosion happened a little while ago. This is just horrible. I've not dealt with death in this way. I've always been lucky and was never close to anyone. At least, not since my parents' death." Marine put her head in her hands and began to sob. She heard Aunt Betsy move and felt tender arms wrap around her shoulders.

"When do you have to go in to work?" Aunt Betsy walked over to the sink, put more water in the teakettle, and turned on the gas stove's eye. She handed Marine a box of tissues. "I'll make some more tea."

"Not until seven. Wayne said it would take them that long to finish putting out the resulting fire. Then, they have to try to determine if they have found all of the bodies. Doing an underwater search won't make much difference if it is daylight or dark. Oh, I'm heartbroken. They were such good folks. The Thomas' were going to take their sailboat back down to Florida next week and sail to the Caribbean soon." Marine buried her head in her arms and continued to cry. Aunt Betsy sat down beside Marine and wrapped her arms around Marine's shoulders, again.

* * * * *

"Damn!" Aunt Jeannie slammed her fist down on the table. The news report of an explosion at the marina mentioned the possibility of four bodies.

"Battalion Chief Wayne Foglesong shared that he and his special unit would be on top of it first light," the reporter said. "The occupants of the sailboat were its owners, Connie and Martin Thomas, and it is believed their friends, Peggy Westbon and Jerry Cline, were also victims. We will report more as we get information from the fire department."

Aunt Jeannie began to pace around her hotel room.

"If I've got something that needs to be done, I need to do it myself. Imbecile! That damn stooge must have set the timer wrong!"

TEN

CONFUSION PLAYS

Arriving early to work, the office atmosphere was somber after the murder of Jerry Cline, a fellow firefighter. Marine managed to walk around several people standing in a group discussing the events of last night. Marine walked over to her desk. The television on the wall was turned up loud enough for all to hear.

The newscast, reporting the most recent details from last night seemed to blare—"Many of the region's firefighters knew Jerry personally. Those that didn't have expressed their sorrow and outrage for the way in which a fellow firefighter has fallen. Many folks here have expressed their grief over the loss of the Thomas', which were both highly regarded as well as Peggy Westbon. All who knew her loved her. She and Jerry were engaged and were planning a fall wedding. As more details come in, we will pass the information on to you. Please stay tuned to WSDJ Channel Three. I'm Nestine Bossom, reporting live at the Evansham Marina."

Chief Altizer walked over to the television and turned it off. He turned around and spoke so all could hear. "Listen up, folks. This latest arson is a hard one for all of us. Many of us knew Jerry and Peggy. We will not let any arsonist get by with any fire. But, I'm sure you join with me in saying, this one is personal. I have armbands for you to wear. We will offer a moment of silence for Jerry, Peggy, and the Thomas', and then let's get this bastard."

Marine walked over, took an armband, and looked down at her hands. They were trembling. She couldn't shake the feeling that this was not the same arsonist. She couldn't express to anyone how she knew it wasn't. It was personal to her. She was anxious to know what was used to trigger the explosion. Wayne said it would be another couple of hours before they would be sure that they had found the detonator. She could just about tell him what it was. She had used one on more than one occasion, always for a boat, and always when it was moored. Last night she didn't want to mention her worst fear to Aunt Betsy, but she was afraid Ana-Geliza was not dead after all. Like the tilted bottle trick, the knapsack or backpack detonator at the hull of a boat was another one of her signature devices. She prayed Wayne and his crew did not find one.

"Hello, Marine." Marine turned around and her mouth dropped open. "Well, aren't you the funny one? Are you trying to catch flies with that open mouth?" Matt said as he took his seat at his desk. "That was bad about the explosion last night."

"What are you doing here?"

"I work here. Or, at least I did last night. Has something changed?"

"No. No, it hasn't. But, you called me last night."

"I did?" Matt riffled through some papers on his desk. "Did we talk? I'm sorry if I seem a little goofy. I didn't get much sleep last night."

"No. We didn't talk, but you said you were headed to Rockbridge County today and wouldn't be in. Did things change?"

"Yes. Yes, they did. I don't know why I told you that. I guess I didn't call back, did I?"

"It doesn't matter. I'm glad you're in today. With everything that is happening, we sure could use you. Did you bring that puzzle piece in with you? Oh, and, before I forget, here, Aunt Betsy sent this just for you. She made them special."

Matt stood up. "You know what? I didn't. I don't like those rolls. You can have them, if you like. I'll go get it and be right back. Man, my lack of sleep is really causing me some problems. I'll be back as soon as I head home and get my evidence bag. I took it inside the house last night." Matt walked out as quickly as he could, not stopping to talk with anyone along the way.

Charles walked up, "Was that Matt?"

"Yes. And, he was acting a little strange. He said he didn't want the cinnamon roll that Aunt Betsy made special for him. But, more importantly, he said that he took his evidence bag inside his house last night. Have you ever known Matt to do that?"

"No. I can't say that I have. And, I've never known him to turn down a cinnamon roll, no matter who made it."

Marine looked in the direction Matt had walked. She wondered if she was on edge from the explosion the previous night. Am I looking for out-of-ordinary things? "Well, I don't know about you, but Matt spooked me just now. It was like it wasn't him."

"You know. When I mentioned to Matt about not showing up at the bar, he was really defensive about it. He said he had not seen you and had no idea where you got the idea that he was going to show up. Then, Fish said he saw him walking into a hooker bar. I thought Matt was going to punch him. He told Fish and me that he would never visit a hooker bar. He got real upset."

"Something is terribly wrong. He is acting like he is walking on egg shells around us."

Tom walked up. "What are you talking about so intently?"

"Matt. He called me last night and left a message about a puzzle piece he found at the fire scene on the north end of the county."

"The outbuilding arson fire?" Charles asked.

"Yes, that's the one. He said he would not be in today as he had a family matter he had to take care of in Rockbridge County. He also said that the puzzle piece had a message written on the back. He was about to tell me what it was when his phone must have gone dead as the call abruptly hung up. He'd warned me earlier in the call that his battery was low."

"Now, he shows up today and is doing weird stuff." Charles added.

"Like what?"

"Have you ever known Matt to take evidence home?"

"No. We all know we can't do that. We must bring it back here no matter how late and place it in the evidence depository until Charles can log it and lock it up properly."

"Precisely. Matt just left to go get his evidence bag that he said he left at home."

Charles looked over at Matt's desk. "I think we should keep a close eye on him. You know, he told us about how he'd put puzzle pieces on paper and store them in the boxes when he thinks that a piece is missing. I'm not saying that Matt is our arsonist, but I'm telling you, it is mighty strange that he seemed to know all about it. I hope I'm wrong."

"I do, too." Marine picked up her notebook. "Tom, I'm going into the processing room and see what I can find out about these latest fires by reading the reports. Will you join me? Charles, if you happen to see Matt come back in, will you come get me?"

A Time for Fire

"Sure, Letsco. Will do." Charles walked to the evidence room.

"Give me about five minutes and I'll be in there to help you with those reports. I have some paperwork I must file from a fire I investigated on Friday. It wasn't an arson fire. I felt sorry for the family that lost their home, but it was nice to know it was an accidental fire and not an arsonist at work."

"Okay. I'll go ahead and get started." Marine picked up the reports sitting at the corner desk and carried them back to the processing room. Besides the fire that Matt was investigating, there were three more that would need to be confirmed as arson or some other cause. She sat down at a table and opened the first folder.

She began to read aloud the report written by Battalion Chief Jack Andre. Marine had learned long ago that she absorbed what she read best if she also heard it spoken:

> Five stations were called out to battle a fire that destroyed a commercial block and injured three people in north New Brook at address: 1125 Ulster Avenue.
> Forty firefighters were called to battle the blaze for the four-alarm fire at oh-eight fifty-four.

Chestnut Mountain Station Three led by Captain Sam Bottoms was the first responding unit.

Four people were taken to Evansham Regional Medical Center; their conditions are unknown at the time of preparing this report. No firefighter injuries were reported. Salvage operations were conducted at the request of Captain Bottoms.

The fire broke out in a building that houses multiple businesses. The initial report from the firefighters say the fire apparently started in the Vinton Check Cashing and Loan business. Fire extension was facilitated by construction breaches in the firewalls or the absence of firewalls.

Fire ground tactics were employed to attack the blaze from outside because of a second floor collapse. Adjacent businesses were evacuated and master streams were employed to protect these exposures. Approximately one dozen people were removed from the burning businesses.

Captain Bottoms was directed by me to send the fire incident report promptly to my office. After several hours, I called Chestnut Mountain Station only to learn that Station Three was still on the scene. I went to the fire scene on Ulster Avenue and found the firefighters of Station Three were still conducting extensive and excessive overhaul of the fire scene. I ordered an immediate halt to their work. I then ordered Chief Bottoms to go to his station and prepare the fire incident report immediately. Next, I ordered LT James and Sergeant Rogers to pack up and return to the station. I will be conducting an inquiry into why Captain Bottoms was doing this unapproved action.

Signed: Battalion Chief Jack Andre.

Marine looked up as Tom walked in. "Do you realize we finally have definitive proof that Captain Bottoms has been shermanizing our work?"

"Really?"

"Battalion Chief Jack Andre is the one filing the claim." Marine handed Tom the report. "Read for yourself."

"This is a bad thing for the fire service." Tom put the paper down. He walked over to the boxes. "I wonder what else is going on here that we don't know. These arson fires are getting worse and more often."

"The only way we're going to find this guy is to keep looking." Marine and Tom began to sift through the boxes.

* * * * *

Aunt Jeannie paced up and down her room at The Edith. She was furious. Damn, Marine. She stopped, looked out the window at the city landscape, and could see Ana-Geliza's smiling face. The last few months, Ana-Geliza had told her many times that Marine was a turncoat agent.

She wished Marine was standing there before her. She'd tell her, "You're like your two-faced Grandma Betsy Lanter. I'm going to enjoy watching you both die." She would see to it that Marine found out the truth just before she died. She's going to learn how Aunt Betsy set her up to be turned into a killing machine by putting her in my care.

"And, I know just where to start." Aunt Jeannie gathered her gun and case.

* * * * *

Carrying groceries, Aunt Betsy walked into the kitchen and placed the bags on the counter. She turned and saw Aunt Jeannie with a gun pointed directly at her.

"Sit down!" Aunt Jeannie walked closer to Aunt Betsy and placed her gun at eye level.

Aunt Betsy walked toward the cabinet to retrieve a hidden weapon.

"You might as well sit down. I've already gotten your gun out of the cabinet. You always were a creature of habit."

Aunt Betsy sat down. "You hear to finish our unfinished business?"

"No. I'm here to deal with the turncoat granddaughter of an agent, Marine."

"What are you going to do?"

"What I do best and enjoy. Killing."

Aunt Betsy looked out the window. "Why don't you finish me off and let it end here? Marine's innocent and you've been fed lies." Aunt Betsy looked at Aunt Jeannie. "Ana-Geliza was jealous of Marine and told you nothing but stories to help her look better than she was."

Aunt Jeannie moved to a chair. "I don't believe anything you're saying. You'll tell lies yourself in order to save that precious granddaughter of yours."

"Why have you come here to tell me this?"

"So, when you're looking at her cold dead body, you'll know you couldn't prevent Marine's death, as righteous and mighty as you always thought you were—you were powerless in the end to save your own blood." Aunt Jeannie rose from her seat. "You know the drill. No use trying to find any of your other guns.

You don't know what I found and what I've done and how long I was in here before you got home. Think about what I said. We'll meet again one day."

Aunt Jeannie walked out leaving Aunt Betsy sitting in her kitchen tapping her fingers on the table. She began to wonder how she could protect Marine. How am I going to take out Aunt Jeannie? Do I handle this myself?

She considered her options and figured that she should call Drake to help her take care of the situation. Aunt Betsy stood up, walked over to the cabinet where she kept her gun, finding it still in its hiding place. She realized Aunt Jeannie had counted on her to be cooperative for Marine's sake. Aunt Jeannie must want Marine to learn about my past, she thought. Drake will be my calling card—my plan B.

ELEVEN

PUZZLING TIMES

Marine and Wayne continued walking the fire scene of the Thomas' sailboat explosion.

"This scene is different from the ones we've seen before with 'Randle the Candle'." Marine watched Wayne pick up more debris and move it over to the side of the dock.

They continued to walk the dock looking at what was left of the sailboat. It had taken a couple of days for all of the debris to be recovered; a crane was used to put it on the dock area to conduct the investigation. All loose debris that was floating had been recovered and numbered to show where it may have originated.

"I was thinking the same thing," Marine said as she motioned to the side of the sailboat that had a gaping hole. "Based on the way this entire section was blown inward, it looks like the explosive device was placed here on the side."

Marine and Wayne continued to study the pieces of the boat. She bent down, looked at a few of the splintered pieces more closely, and thought this couldn't be the work of 'Randle the Candle'. This was not matching his style.

"Wayne, you know, my past experience tells me that this was done by an expert."

"I was afraid you'd say that," Wayne walked over to her. "What do we do now?"

"I'm not sure. But, whoever did this wanted to make sure it was a kill. I'm wondering who in the world's done this and why." Marine pulled out her cell. "I think I will call Aunt Betsy. Something tells me she might need me." Marine listened to the phone ring, but there was no answer.

* * * * *

By noon, they had completed their initial investigation. Marine wanted to get back to reading the arson reports. She told Wayne the sailboat explosion would have to wait. She needed to focus on one problem right now. She

A Time for Fire

felt she was close but was missing something important. Back at her office, she began to settle into studying the fire reports.

Tom Willard handed Marine another stack of fire reports. "These are the last ones. When we finish, we will have read through all of them dating back as far as our records are kept. Some of the older records were lost due to a water leak at the old station."

After spending hours reading, Marine motioned to Tom. "Come here. Let me read this one to you."

> When West Evansham Fire Station One responded to the scene, a duplex located at 12300 block of West Viewpoint Drive, shortly before 0500 hours, the duplex was engulfed in flames. After bringing the fire under control, it was initially determined that the blaze had apparently started on the front porch. The damage was called moderate; while police on the scene called it extensive—and determined it was deliberately set and a total loss.
>
> Four or five people were in the home as the blaze started after a reported altercation between the owner and a visitor along with a few other people. One person suffered minor injuries.

"Let's see what the evidence bag holds," Tom said. Marine handed it to him. He laid several pieces of debris that were scorched onto the table. It was easy to still make out that the objects had been laying around the house when the fire occurred. As Tom pulled items from the bag, he pulled out a folded piece of paper.

"Marine, look here. Now, how do you suppose that piece of paper managed to not be scorched like the rest of the contents?"

"You know, Tom, this paper was added after the fact. It couldn't have survived that fire the way this looks and according to the eyewitness accounts. Besides, the building ended up being a total loss."

Tom began to open the folded paper as a puzzle piece fell to the table.

"We've been looking at this all wrong, Tom. These puzzle pieces were planted. They weren't from the actual fire scene. Someone wants us to think they were."

"How is that possible? Charles wouldn't let anyone into the evidence room."

"I'm afraid it is Matt. It has to be. He's the only one that has said anything to us about puzzle pieces. You remember how he said he would tape puzzle pieces to paper to help him find where the piece goes?"

Tom shook his head. "I can't believe it. Why would he implicate himself? He wouldn't. I know it."

"We have over thirty pieces here. If all of these were planted, then who did it? It has to be one of our own. The only person we know who comes close is Matt, unless it is you or me."

"I just don't know. I mean, we're talking about Matt, here. Matt saved my life more than once when we served in the same station. Come on, Marine. You've got to be wrong."

"I agree it is hard to swallow that. Let's look at this last arson fire. If there is a puzzle piece included, then will you be willing to at least consider it is Matt?"

"Yes. I will, but I don't like it."

Tom and Marine pulled out the evidence from the last of the arson evidence boxes they were investigating. When they found the puzzle piece, Tom was not happy.

"I'm telling you, Marine. This ain't right. It just ain't right."

"What's not right?" Charles asked as he came into the processing lab.

"All evidence is pointing to someone from within placing evidence—these puzzle pieces—as part of past arson fires. We believe it might be Matt." Marine pointed to the puzzle pieces on the table.

"Have you tried putting the puzzle pieces together to see if they fit?" Charles walked over to the table and looked at them closer.

"No. We haven't yet. We just figured out that these had been recently planted."

"That's impossible," Charles turned back and looked at Tom and Marine.

"Don't get excited, Charles. We're not saying you did it. We're saying that Matt did it."

"But, why?" Charles looked to Tom. "Why would he do that to his career? He's so close to retirement now."

"Actually, Charles, I'm not saying it. Marine is. She's convinced it's him. I'm not so sure."

"Well, who else? It's not me. Is it one of you two?" Charles said as he pointed his fingers at them.

"No, it's not." Marine walked over to the puzzle pieces. "Let's do what you said, Charles. Let's see if these pieces fit. They do look like they might belong to the same puzzle now that I'm looking at them for that purpose."

A Time for Fire

Tom's cell phone rang. He stepped away. Marine and Charles began trying to piece the puzzle together. Little snippets of a scene began to take shape.

"You won't believe who just called me?" Tom said as he walked back into the room.

"Who?" Charles said as he placed another puzzle piece.

"Matt's ex-wife. She said she hadn't heard from him in over three weeks. She said even though they were split that he still cared for her. She was worried."

Marine looked down at the puzzle pieces taking shape. "Did you tell her he was in here not long ago?"

"Yes, but, I'm not sure she believed me. It was strange."

"This is obviously the beginning of a puzzle of a fire scene. Now that these two—Oh my God!" Marine dropped the pieces when she saw the words take shape.

"What's wrong?" Charles asked as he picked up the dropped pieces. "I see letters on some of these pieces."

"What do they say?" Tom asked. "I'll write it on the white board as you call it out."

"'Ran' is on one. Another one is 'the' with a space, and then 'Can', and the last one has the letter 't' by itself followed by 'Pik'."

"Does it look like this?" Tom stood back.

Ran   the   Can   t Pik

"Yes. What do you make of that?"

"I know what it means. It says, "Randle the Candle is Matt Pike." Marine looked solemn. "I think we need to tell Chief Altizer now. It needs to be looked into."

"Yes. It does need to be looked into," Tom said. "Suppose it says something different?"

Charles said, "I'll get the Chief."

About five minutes later, Chief Altizer and Charles came back into the processing lab. The team updated the Chief on their findings.

Chief Altizer stood there with a concerned look on his face. "I'll contact internal affairs. This has to stay quiet. Is that understood?" They all nodded in agreement. Chief Altizer left the room.

"Now, we have that investigation going. It should take a couple of days to find out what we need to know regarding Matt and his prior history."

"Let's put the rest of the pieces together to see what we get." Tom began arranging the pieces as best as possible. "I think it may help us find out what is going on with this puzzle."

Marine stood back and looked at the resulting picture. The scene showed part of a barn and what looked like the boom arm of a nozzle truck fighting a fire with a yellow and orange blaze burning around an old out building. The four pieces with the lettering: Ran the Can t Pik fit perfectly off to the bottom edge where it could form the bottom right corner. The final corner piece was missing. Marine figured it would have an 'e' on it. The other pieces missing she felt in her heart would complete the phrase.

"I'm having a hard time with this. Does anyone recognize where this barn might be located or, better yet, remember a fire at a scene like this?" Marine pointed to the barn that showed a light pole standing in front of it. Off to the left of the building on fire, there appeared to be the beginning of another out building. There were high grasses along the bottom edge of the puzzle scene with the tail end of what looked like a camper off to the right just out of view.

"No, but you know who might?" Charles offered.

"Who?"

"Fish or some of the other guys at your old fire house. Why don't we have them come over and ask them? They are some of the 'senior old heads' that we can rely on for knowing the facts of an old fire scene."

"Marine, I think Charles has given us a good place to start. I'll feel better if we did what we could to make sure Matt's in the clear on this."

"Tom, I'm with you there. And you know what else?" Tom and Charles looked at Marine with interest. "With this arsonist and the sailboat explosion, I think we have two diabolical criminals amongst us." She picked up her note pad. "Let's see what we can find out."

TWELVE

....

DANGER LURKS

"Chet? Is that you?" Aunt Betsy called from the back room of her pantry. "I hope it's you." She walked out into the kitchen.

"Yes. It is me. I called back to you twice, but I think you were so far into that room you call a pantry you could not hear me. I came as soon as I got your message. What's up?" Chet walked over and gave Aunt Betsy a hug. "You sounded worried on your voice mail."

"I am, Chet. It's plain and simple. Have a seat. Have you had lunch?" Aunt Betsy walked over to the counter and placed two canning jars into the deep bowl of her sink. "I've gotten some fresh tomatoes. I thought I'd blanch them, and then can them while we talk."

"Aunt Betsy, slow down. I am free to be here all afternoon if you need me to stay. I cleared my calendar when I heard your voice. Now, sit down and explain to me what has gotten you so upset. You do not go to canning in the middle of the day unless you are upset. What has happened?"

"You're right." Aunt Betsy took a seat, and then popped right up out of her chair. "I can't sit just yet. Have you eaten? You didn't tell me."

"Yes. I had lunch before I heard your voice mail. Again, I am fine. I tell you what. You sit down here. I will fix us both some tea. How is that?" Chet maneuvered Aunt Betsy toward her chair. She watched as he worked. He put water in the teakettle, placed it on the stove, and then he carried the cups to the table and set them before Aunt Betsy. "You examine them and make sure I have the right teabags in the cups."

Chet sat in his chair and asked, "Okay. Now, explain. It will take the water another ten minutes before it is ready to pour. You can tell me a lot of things in that time." He smiled.

"You're right. I can't seem to get my mind around this whole thing. It's such a nightmare. I will lose her for sure when she finds out."

"Aunt Betsy, I know you think I am a whiz at helping people. And, quite frankly, I hope I am. But, I have no idea what or whom you are talking about. Would you start at the beginning?"

"I'll try. But, Chet, you have to promise me one thing. You won't breathe a word of this to anyone. You promise?"

Chet took hold of Aunt Betsy's hand. He patted it softly. "I promise."

Aunt Betsy smiled and hoped he was being honest. Of course, she never knew him not to tell her the truth. She took a deep breath.

"Aunt Jeannie is in town."

"Aunt Betsy." Chet looked down at the table. He looked up at Aunt Betsy and smiled. "Who is Aunt Jeannie?"

"Oh, my. I've never told you about her?"

"No. Not that I recall."

"This is going to be harder than I thought. Well, let me see. I feel so lost. But, we can't tell Marine. You promise me. Not a word."

"Okay. I promise."

"Her full name is Jean Bathroy. She and I first met when I worked in Washington, D. C. many years ago. At one point, we were best of friends. That went away a long time ago. Now, you could say we are mortal enemies. I'm afraid that I'm going to have to kill her."

The teakettle began to send out a loud whistle. "Hold that thought for a minute." Chet got up and retrieved the teapot, turning off the gas to the stove's eye. He poured the hot water over the tea bags and slipped a tea cozy over each cup. "Okay. Now, let me see if I have this straight. Aunt Jeannie was a dear friend of yours and now, because of something that has happened that you have not shared with me yet; you are going to kill her? Have I got that right?"

Aunt Betsy smiled. "I guess it does sound a little crazy. But, yes, you have it right. She must die."

"I have dealt with a lot of problems that people have brought to me. I do not remember having someone tell me in advance that they were going to kill someone. Are you sure this is not anger getting the best of you? I mean you do not kill people."

This time, Aunt Betsy caressed Chet's hand. "Oh, Chet, I must correct you. I have and will do so when it means my family is in danger. Aunt Jeannie means to kill Marine. I can't have that happen. You understand?"

"You killed someone? Who?"

"It's enough for you to know that I have killed for my job. I will tell you more later. You have to understand what is at stake here. Do you?"

"Well, of course. We will go to the police and have them take Aunt Jeannie into custody. We can protect Marine without killing someone. How do you know she means to kill Marine anyway?"

"She was in this house a few days ago when I came in with the groceries. She told me what she planned to do and that there was nothing I was going to be able to do to stop her. She is wrong. Drake is coming to town and he will help me."

"Drake?"

"Yes. Drake is my support. He will be my eyes. I had to call him and ask him for a favor. We are old friends from my days at the INR.

"INR? What was that?"

"I worked for an agency of the federal government when I was younger. I was involved in work that resulted in me meeting malicious people. I also met many people who worked hard to keep the world safe and protected. That's how I met Drake. It is where I first learned about how the necessity to do a job may involve doing things that do not match with one's beliefs. Along the way, I made friends and I made enemies. We have to protect Marine at all costs. Drake is very much aware of the link between Marine and Aunt Jeannie. He has kept me informed over the last few years about her whereabouts as well as how Aunt Jeannie was treating her before she went on the cruise. Drake was on the cruise to keep an eye on Marine."

"What? Did he know I was your adopted nephew?"

"No. I didn't tell him that right away. I only asked him to keep an eye on Marine when he told me she would be going on the same cruise with you."

"But, wait a minute. You knew she was going to be on the cruise? How did you know Marine before? I did not know anything about her."

"It's a long story. Right now, I need you to understand that I will indeed kill Aunt Jeannie if she forces my hand. I tried to reason with her the other day, but she was insistent that she was going to harm Marine."

"I know from working with Marine and her memory loss, she never let on that she knew you before. Did she?"

"No."

"Did she know Drake before?"

"I'm not sure. I think she may have seen him at some point during her career as an assassin, but I don't think she ever met him until she met him on the cruise ship."

"I have got to ask, how do you know Marine?"

"Please, Chet, allow me to wait and tell you later. I can't deal with Marine finding out now. Right now, I have to focus on keeping her alive and safe. Can you understand?"

"I can if you tell me one thing. When I called to ask you about bringing Marine home, did you already know that she was the same person Drake was watching? And, did you set me up to meet her on the ship? And, if so, when were you going to tell me?"

"Chet, I'm sorry if I've hurt you by not telling you this before. I hadn't planned on anyone ever knowing. Yes. I knew it was Marine. I did not set you up to meet. Her accident ended up being a blessing for me to get to see her. I had hoped I would not need to tell you or Marine, for that matter. Aunt Jeannie coming to town has changed all of that now."

"Can you explain one thing to me?"

"Sure."

"Why do you call each other Aunt Jeannie and Aunt Betsy?"

"That's really a funny story. It started back in our INR days. We were doing some work with an orphanage in a foreign country. The children were told to call us Aunt. Jean and I started calling each other that, and it just stuck. Over the years, the nickname became the names we used."

"Okay. So, then, why does Aunt Jeannie want Marine dead? Did Marine kill one of her family members?"

"No, I don't think so. But, I do know Aunt Jeannie is deranged."

"That is all the more reason we should call the police."

"I know. But, when Drake gets here, we can talk with him about it. Our tea is getting cold. Do you want any cream or would you like me to warm your cup up?"

"Aunt Betsy, you are trying to change the subject and it will not work. And, no, my tea is fine. I will let it be if you are going to tell me later. I have not known this long. I can wait to hear the entire story when you are ready to tell me. Now, why did you call me? Do you want me to do something?"

"Can Drake stay at your place?"

* * * * *

Drake stepped out of the cab and got his bag. He didn't think he would be back in town this soon. He walked up the steps to Chet's apartment. Aunt Betsy was always good about giving directions that were concise and easy to follow. He knocked on Chet's door.

The door opened. Aunt Betsy greeted Drake with a smile.

"Well, I didn't expect I'd be greeting such a pretty face. Is Chet here?" Drake stepped in and gave Aunt Betsy a hug.

"I am in the kitchen. Would you like something to drink?"

"Yes, scotch on the rocks. It was a long flight from London." He walked over to Chet and offered his hand to shake. Chet wiped his hands on his apron before shaking Drake's hand. "I know it sounds funny, me being an MI6 agent, but we don't get to ride in first class like they portray in those Bond movies. I had to sit in between two real talkative sorts. It made for a very long flight." Chet handed him his drink.

"Aunt Betsy, would you like a drink?" Chet stepped out into the living room. "I have your favorite."

"Yes, then, I will." Chet brought her a cold Naty Light poured in a frosted glass. He motioned to Drake to take a seat as he took off his apron. Chet sat down cradling his drink.

"What are you having, Chet?" Drake asked as he sat down.

"Bourbon and coke. My standby."

"I guess we can get down to business," Aunt Betsy said as she took a sip. "What do you hear about Jean Bathroy or Aunt Jeannie as I call her?" Aunt Betsy said as she stretched out her legs.

"Just before I left this morning, we received word that she was coming to New Brook."

"As I told you yesterday, I was worried about her and needed your help. She's here already and has been evidently for almost a week. That's why I called in a favor."

Drake looked concerned. "That changes things."

"Yes, it does. She was waiting for me in my house a few days ago when I came in with my groceries. She promised me that she would be taking Marine out."

"She has gotten blatant in her old age."

"Careful. I'm the same age." Aunt Betsy smiled.

Drake looked her over. He wondered if she was worried about her strength and agility. He wouldn't ask her. Not now. Not when so much was at stake.

"What are you thinking?" Chet asked. Drake looked up. He realized he needed to be extra careful around Chet until he knew him better.

"How much does Marine know?" Drake leaned forward. "I guess Chet knows everything?"

"No. Chet does not know everything. I have been told that one day I will. Besides, I think I will leave you two to talk. I have patients who confide in me and trust me. I will be back later. Make yourself at home, Drake. You know where everything is I am sure already." Chet picked up his briefcase and went out the door.

"Did I upset him by coming here?"

"No. I did. I had not told him about the cruise and he still doesn't know that Marine is my granddaughter. Neither does Marine."

"Is that wise?"

"It is what it is for now. Besides, I'm glad Chet is gone. We can talk more freely. I need to tell you about Marine and Wayne anyway." Drake frowned. "They are beginning to get serious. If you want to make your move, you need to do it while you're here this time. I'm not sure you will have a chance if you don't."

"Here we are getting ready to plot the murder of your best friend and you're thinking about love at a time like this." They laughed.

* * * * *

Aunt Jeannie paced the floor of her new room in The Edith. The view from her room overlooked the north side of town. She could almost make out Aunt Betsy's house sitting on the hill in the distance. The summer moonlight shone down on the town giving it a glow on the late summer night. She thought to herself how she should have kidnapped Marine when she had the chance the other night, but she was too busy trying to impress Aunt Betsy. "It was stupid of me," she said to herself.

A Time for Fire

She heard a knock at her door. Aunt Jeannie wasn't expecting anyone. She looked at the clock on her nightstand. It was almost one. Looking through the camera peephole in her door, she read, 'Open the door, or I'll blow you down through it.' Aunt Jeannie knew that it was Aunt Betsy, and it wasn't a joke. Her gun sat on the desk, across the room. She opened the door.

"Come on in, Betsy. So good to see you this evening."

"It's almost morning. Step back. I'll close the door."

Aunt Betsy surveyed the room. The dresser top had the ingredients for a brandy shake. "Did you bring your usual flask of cognac or did you settle for whiskey?" Jeannie picked up the flask. "Is that the same flask I gave you when we were friends?"

"Yes. It served me well then, as it does now. What brings you here at this hour?"

"Surprised? I figured you'd forgotten the old trick with the sign at the door we used to play on each other. It always worked for me. You seemed to never remember how it should play out to your advantage."

"Are you here to bring up old stories or do you have something to say?"

"I have plenty to say. Take a seat. It won't take long. I don't trust you standing." Jeannie started to walk over toward her desk. "No, not there. I see you left your gun on the desk. You sit on the bed."

Betsy walked over to the desk keeping her gun pointed at Jeannie. She picked up Jeannie's gun and placed it in her bag.

"You won't need this anytime soon."

"You know I can get another one."

"Yes, I know. But, right now, you don't have one within easy reach. That's all that matters to me."

"Okay. What do you want?"

"I want to make sure you understand that this old feud is between you and me. No one else. You leave Marine alone."

"Seems like I've got you running scared."

"No. I'm being fair by warning you. I'm throwing the gauntlet down. You hurt a single small fiber of Marine—her hair, her clothes, her job—and I'll kill you. Do I make myself clear?"

"Sure. But, why should I listen?"

"We were friends once. I'd like for us to remain so, but you've managed to change that by sending Ana-Geliza after Marine. I took care of that. Ana-Geliza will not hurt anyone ever again. Now, I will be cordial to you. I might even smile at you. I can't say we can be friends as we once were, but I am willing to stop this here and now if you are."

"What did you do to Ana-Geliza?"

"Oh, you're interested. That lovely girl didn't have a prayer up against me. You should know that by now. I took my usual trophy."

"You killed her!"

"Yes."

Jeannie lunged at Betsy. The woman reacted by hitting Jeannie over the head with her gun causing her to fall hard to the floor. She was knocked out cold. Betsy looked through the woman's things making sure she had found all of her weapons.

Taking two more that were stashed in her belongings, she tied up Jeannie to make sure that she would not be able to follow her. Slyly, Betsy slipped out of the hotel.

About an hour later, Jeannie began to come around. She cried out in anger, "Oh, my precious daughter, Ana-Geliza!"

THIRTEEN

A DARK HORSE

The last three days had been long and hard for Marine pulling fourteen and fifteen hours of work each day. Marine didn't know the last time she'd talked with Aunt Betsy or Chet. As she finished dressing, she gathered her bag and note pad. She'd been making notes about the results found regarding the most recent arson fires and the additional puzzle pieces. She decided to stop by Aunt Betsy's for a cup of coffee. She knew she hadn't visited with her since the boat explosion. She wondered what was going on with her dear friend.

Marine walked up the back steps noticing that the door was open. It was unusual for this time of the morning. Carefully, Marine opened the back-screened door making sure it didn't creak too much. She hoped a prowler wasn't inside. She walked slowly around the kitchen and stopped to listen. Silence. She looked out at the garage. It was open and Aunt Betsy's car was gone. Marine dialed Aunt Betsy's cell. She could hear a faint ring coming from the upstairs. She made her way upstairs, again stepping with caution to avoid making noise. She could still hear the cell phone ringing. I hope I don't find her on the floor, Marine thought as she walked into Aunt Betsy's bedroom.

As she surveyed the room, the cell went to voice mail and dinged a familiar tune as it went silent. Marine walked to the bed where it lay and picked it up. She checked and noticed the last two calls to Aunt Betsy were her calls. She carried the phone over to the dresser to call Chet. Something glistened from the sun's rays beaming through the window and caught her eye. She moved her hand back and forth and saw that the sparkle of light grew in intensity depending on how the light reflected off her silver bracelet. The sparkle of light was coming from a slightly opened box sitting on the dresser.

A Time for Fire

Turning to open the box, she found it full of delicate pieces of jewelry; on top set an ornate broach. Marine had a sudden flash back. She was playing jump rope with a group of girls one cold winter day. A lady dressed in a heavy overcoat got out of a black sedan, then walked up to them. The lady smiled and nodded her head. Marine felt she should know her, but couldn't quite make out why. The lady turned to walk away as Aunt Jeannie called to her. Marine saw the pin on her coat catching the sun's rays. As she looked down at the brooch in her hand, she realized it was the same pin—that lady was Aunt Betsy.

Marine took the brooch over to the desk and sat down. She turned it over and over in her hands. She looked at it carefully. There was something about it that she couldn't remember, but she knew she'd seen the brooch before she saw it on Aunt Betsy's coat. It was a gilded pin inlaid with a bald eagle engraved in exquisite detail. Along the outer edge, in a half circle pattern, a cluster of rubies and pearls finished the design. The ornateness of the brooch reminded her of a dignitary's insignia or something that could have been used by the military.

Marine stood up, walked back to the dresser, and placed the brooch in the box. As she did so, her finger pressed up against a button she didn't see before. A side compartment opened. Marine looked inside and saw a lock of hair. She opened the side compartment further only to reveal seven additional locks of hair. The largest one was about six inches long made of dark ebony hair wrapped tightly in a braid and clamped together with a tortoise shell barrette. Marine turned it over in her fingers. There was no label or tag. It looked familiar. She had a feeling it belonged to someone she once knew.

"Why is this in here?" she said aloud. Marine decided to put everything back as she found it. She wouldn't confront Aunt Betsy about what she found until she had more time to think it all through. She wasn't sure what it all meant, but she knew that Aunt Betsy was more of a dark horse than she could imagine.

Marine walked down the stairs and the front door opened. It was Aunt Betsy.

"Is there something you needed?" Aunt Betsy said as she set her packages on the chair at the door.

"Good morning. Where have you been?"

A Time for Fire

"Oh, the grocery store. As you can see, I bought a few things."

"Kind of early to be out."

"I wanted to get my shopping done before it got too hot. You know, the July heat can get you down. If you're going into work today, you need your raincoat. They're calling for some unexpected showers and heavy downpours." Aunt Betsy set her purse down, and then picked up her bags. Marine followed her into the kitchen. "Are you working today?"

"Yes. I had stopped by for some early morning coffee. But, since you weren't here, I tried calling your cell. I heard your cell ring upstairs, so I went to make sure you were okay. You are okay, aren't you?"

Aunt Betsy set the bags on the counter. She tapped her fingers on the counter and looked back at Marine. "Yes, I'm fine. You shouldn't be worrying about me while you have an arsonist on the loose. I heard about the new fires. Anymore news about the marina explosion?"

"No."

"I would have called you, but my phone's battery died. I figured I'd get to see you soon, but didn't realize you'd be by so early this morning or I would have waited before I went out."

Marine stood there and watched Aunt Betsy put up her small bag of groceries. She wondered if Aunt Betsy believed that she was getting away with her evasive maneuvering. It wasn't working. I wanted to ask her where she'd been as I didn't believe she'd gone out early only to grocery shop.

"I do need to head on into the office. We have been working for days non-stop on the investigation of the latest arson fires as well as the sailboat explosion."

"Oh, of course. I was wondering. Have you heard anything about a memorial service for the Thomas' or the other two?"

"Jerry and Peggy?" Aunt Betsy nodded her head. "No. I know that the bodies haven't been released from the morgue after the autopsies. I'd say we should hear something in the next day or so, if not sooner. Why do you ask?"

"I thought I'd go with you when you pay your respects."

"I really haven't given it much thought. I know that sounds horrid. Work has me burning the candle on both ends." Marine chuckled to herself.

A Time for Fire

"What's so funny?" Aunt Betsy looked serious as Marine looked up.

"Nothing really. I just said burning the candle. We have this arsonist we've dubbed 'Randle the Candle.' Actually, he called himself that in one of his letters. I guess it was sick of me to giggle. I am that tired."

"You head on off to work and plan to come home early. I'll make your favorite dinner. How's that?"

"That sounds good. I'll probably be ready to talk with you then, too. We have some catching up to do." Marine closed the door behind her as she saw Aunt Betsy walking upstairs.

FOURTEEN

....

CHAOS AND CALM

Reading through her notes and papers she had accumulated working on the 'Randle the Candle' case, Marine couldn't quite figure out why Matt would be in the midst of all of the different fires. Yet, all of the pieces came from the same puzzle. They were able to get an idea of the picture of the same scene as the puzzle. At least, it was close enough. The remaining structure that was depicted as on fire in the puzzle had since been torn down. But, the light pole, mountain range in the background, and the old barn, all matched the puzzle pieces as best Marine and her team could tell. She could not find a connection to Matt and many of the older fires. She was beginning to believe the puzzle pieces were planted to make him look guilty.

Marine looked up at the clock. It was almost ten. She walked over to Matt's desk. She had left him several messages the last few days. Due to her busy schedule, she hadn't realized until then that she hadn't seen him. She walked over to Charles' office in the evidence room and knocked on his door.

"Come on in," Charles said.

Marine walked in. "Got a minute?"

"Sure. What can I do you for?" Charles grinned showing a tooth missing. He had told Marine sometime back that he lost it in a fire when a beam fell down and hit him. He was lucky. His partner got pinned and before he could be recused, both his legs were severely burned. Charles told her that when people see his missing tooth, he knows they laugh inside while he dies inside remembering his best friend lost both his legs. Marine wondered why he never got the tooth replaced with a bridge or dentures. She figured it was his way of punishing himself for being lucky.

"Have you spoken with Matt lately?"

"No. Actually, I haven't seen him for a week. He called in sick two or three days, and then I was told he had switched his time around and was working the evening shift."

A Time for Fire

"Evening shift? For whom? We don't have an evening shift. We all work the hours we work. You should know that."

"I thought it was strange. I've been so busy I didn't think much about it."

"Okay. I'll go see the Chief. Thanks." Marine started to walk out the door. She turned back. "Did you ever check into getting a bridge for that missing tooth?"

"No. Don't need it."

Marine turned and walked out. Just as I figured, she thought. He's punishing himself. She walked down the corridor and turned right at the end of the hall. She almost walked straight into Tom and some other guy with him.

"There you are. I was telling Archie here that you were always at your desk."

"What ya got?" Marine said noticing that Archie held a thick folder. She stuck out her hand. "Hi, I'm Marine Letsco. You are?"

"Archie. Archie Melton. I'm so glad to meet you. I've heard a lot about you from the guys over at Station Three. You're a legend over there, you know?"

"No. I didn't know. Thanks for telling me. So, Archie Melton, what do you do for the department?"

"He's our head computer geek and researcher," Tom chimed in. "I asked him to bring what he found out about Matt Pike."

"Good. As a matter of fact, I was just heading to see the Chief. I'll be right back." Marine began to walk away. She turned back, "You haven't seen Matt today have you, Tom?"

"No. I haven't seen him for several days."

Marine waved back and walked over to the Chief's office. She knocked on his door.

"Enter." Chief Altizer was on the phone. Marine waited until he finished. "What can I do for you, Letsco?"

"Is Matt Pike still out on sick leave?"

"Sick leave?"

"Yes. Charles said he was told Matt was out on sick leave."

"That's odd. I spoke with Matt twice in the last two days. As far as I could tell, he sounded fine. Letsco, I'm glad you came in. I need to let you know that Captain Bottoms was terminated for severe violation of department policies, and he's damn lucky he wasn't criminally charged for what he did. You and Tom did a hard job, but one that needed doing. Good job."

"Thank you, sir. Sir?"

"Yes?"

"Matt Pike. Sir, I believe that Matt might be involved in the arson—"

"Letsco, you are off your rocker if you are going to try and tell me that Matt is no good. Now, just because you managed to pick it correct on Chief Bottoms, doesn't mean Matt is a bad egg. You need to find yourself another suspect. Now, get back to work. I have more important things to consider."

Marine closed the door and shook her head. This was going to be tough. She walked over to Tom and Archie. "Okay. Well. First, Captain Bottoms has been terminated for violating department policies. Now, what do you have on Matt? Chief Altizer said he just talked with him twice in the last two days. Has anyone seen him?"

Archie opened up his folder and began passing pictures to Tom and Marine. "I haven't seen Matt in years, but these pictures will give you something to think about. Matt has a twin brother."

Marine looked at Tom. He appeared as surprised as she was. Marine began to wonder and said, "A twin? No wonder we've been fooled."

"Well, now, wait a minute. Pat, who is his twin brother's name, was killed when he escaped from prison. He escaped six months ago but was killed only two weeks ago."

"Where had he been held?" Tom asked handing back the photographs to Archie.

"He had been in the Central State Institution for the last twenty years until earlier this year when he broke out. Evidently, Matt had not been told about his brother's breakout. Pat was institutionalized for being a juvenile fire setter. He also had tried to commit murder. He framed Matt at one point. Matt was arrested and charged with the crime. It wasn't until ten days later that proof was provided that it was Pat and not Matt who had committed the crimes."

Tom rubbed his forehead. "I just can't wrap my mind around this. Matt never said a word to me about him having a brother. Let alone, one who had done this. No wonder Matt was such a workaholic. It was as if he could never get the job done."

A Time for Fire

Archie set the folder down. "I'd like to know if Matt has heard about his brother and that's caused him to act differently or depressed."

"Does that mean that Matt is as loopy as his brother?" Marine picked up the folder and looked through it again. She pulled out Matt and Pat's pictures, held them up for Tom and Archie to see. "They are identical twins. Really identical. I wonder if their mother could even tell the difference."

"We haven't found anyone that has seen Matt for the last week. All we have is that the Chief said he talked with him." Tom took Matt's picture from Marine's hand. "I can't believe that Matt is involved in these fires."

"That's Pat's picture," Marine said.

* * * * *

Marine had an appointment at Crystal's Shaping Nail Salon at two. She was due a long lunch break after working two twelve-hour shifts back-to-back. She decided to stop in Flourz for a fruit and berry salad. She loved the poppy seed dressing they used on the spinach and feta cheese. While she waited, she looked out over Tazewell Street. She was marveling at how much work the owner had managed to do in moving her business, Petal's, across the alley. Marine's gaze froze. It can't be, she thought.

"I'll be back," she said as she went out the door. She moved quickly across the street, but tried to keep herself hidden, in case Aunt Jeannie saw her. Damn, I don't have a gun on me. She saw Aunt Jeannie turn down a side entrance behind The Edith. By the time I get around to the front, she'll be gone, Marine thought. I better call Aunt Betsy. She reached for her cell only to realize she'd left it in Flourz. Walking back toward the restaurant, she wondered why Aunt Jeannie would be in town.

"Well, you did come back," said George as he handed Marine her cell phone. "We've got your salad made. Are you taking it with you?"

"Yes, thanks. And, thanks for my cell!" Marine picked up her bag. "I did pay already, right?"

"Yes, on both counts. Enjoy your food."

"Thanks to both of you. I will."

"Come back when you can visit," George's wife, Teresa, called as she continued making sandwiches and other deli orders.

Marine got her cell and dialed Aunt Betsy. The phone rang and rang. No answer again. This is getting old. Marine picked up her bag, walked out the door, and turned to head toward Crystal's.

* * * * *

"Well, hello to you!" Crystal said with a broad smile as Marine sat down on the couch. "You've had a rough one, haven't you?"

"Yes. You could say that. I need a pedicure bad. I wish you did massages, too. I could use a 'Calgon-take-me-away' moment right now."

"Come back in two weeks and I'll have a masseuse."

"You're kidding."

"No. We will even pamper you in such a way that you won't know how to act."

"That sounds divine. Course, the last time I went for a massage, it didn't turn out so well. I may need to set it up to be a whole day experience. You know, a 'Marine Special Spa Day.' Do you think we could work that out?"

"What do you have in mind?" Crystal motioned for Marine to take off her boots to get ready to stick her feet into the foot massage bath.

As Marine took off her shoes, she watched Crystal. While her friend was pouring bath salts into the bubbling water, she hummed along with the oldies song playing in the background. She motioned for Marine to place her feet into the warm, churning water of the footbath. The bubbles lapped up around her ankles while the cushioning massage nodes gently aided in relaxing her feet. "I'm thinking we should do a day of massage coupled with a manicure and pedicure. I could get the royal treatment. Since I'm in a man's world most of the day, this will give me a little femininity to look forward to experiencing once in a while."

Crystal continued getting her pedicure tools ready. "Sounds good to me. We can discuss it more later. For now, I'm going to go take a five-minute break while you soak. You sit back and enjoy this time off your feet."

Marine smiled as Crystal stepped out of the room. Her feet were relaxing. She could feel the tension easing away. She sank back into the pillows. They were the perfect cushions to relax in. Her mind drifted to Aunt Betsy. Marine thought back to when Aunt Betsy told her about a secret love she had when she was younger and her friendship with Aunt Jeannie. As Marine thought about Aunt Betsy's story, she realized that Aunt Betsy never mentioned if she married. I wonder if she had any children.

She never said and neither had Chet. Marine continued to think about what she knew about this woman who was becoming special to her.

"You're in deep thought," Crystal said as Marine jumped.

"Oh. I guess I was."

"The foot bath is doing its job then, good. Work stressing you out?" Crystal positioned herself up against the footbath and motioned to Marine to place her foot up on her lap so that she could begin the pedicure.

"Yes."

"Anything you want to talk about?"

"No, not really." Marine thought some more. "Well, maybe. Do you have any children?"

Crystal laughed. "No. Why?"

"Would you tell anyone if you did have a child out of wedlock?"

"Probably not. Even though, now a days' it's not as big a deal."

"Would you keep the child?"

"I don't know. It depends. I would like to if I had a child. But, sometimes life happens and you can't always do what you want in your heart. You have to do what is right for the child."

"What do you mean?"

"Well, if I didn't have a lot of money. And, if I knew if I gave the child to someone else, the child would have a better life. I think I would at least consider it."

Marine nodded. She thought to the little memory she had of being with her mother and father. She knew they loved her. She could still feel their love. But, where were their parents? Why didn't they take her after her mother and father died? She picked up a magazine and began to pretend she was reading while she still thought about Aunt Betsy. I think I'm going to ask her the same questions I just asked Crystal. It will be interesting to see how she answers. I wonder what the story is about Aunt Jeannie, too.

Crystal had finished prepping Marine's feet and was beginning to paint her toenails. Marine decided she'd give Chet a call.

"Hello, Chet. How are you this afternoon?" Marine smiled at Crystal, who had selected a dark navy blue nail polish. Marine nodded affirmatively for her to paint her toes that color. "Chet, have you talked with Aunt Betsy?" Chet responded that he had and that she was standing right there in his office. "Oh. Good. Would you tell her that I'd like to speak with you both when I get home? And that old friend of hers is in town. I should be done here in another half-hour. I'll call you when I leave. Okay?" Chet tells Marine he will tell Aunt Betsy. "You have a good rest of the afternoon, too, Chet." Marine hung up her cell.

"So, how do you like your toes?"

"I love them. The navy blue will look good with my uniform."

"But, you wear boots. No one will see them."

"I will." Marine hopped down. She sat where she could put her toes in the nail dryer. After ten minutes, she was ready to put on her socks and lace up her boots.

"Let's book me for another pedicure and add a manicure with it in three weeks. These nails are still looking good. I don't have half the damage since I'm not fighting fires anymore. Besides, I love how the gel polish wears."

Marine finished paying Crystal and set up her next appointment. She walked out to her Durango, opened the driver's side door, and placed her pocketbook inside when a fire tone went off. She knew immediately that it would be another suspected arson fire. It was now a habit. Chief Altizer had setup the tone system for the Special Unit in order that all would be notified at the same time to report for duty. The tones finished blaring. Marine looked at her cell for the incoming text. She read—

> This is an all call for the Special Investigative Unit. Suspected arson fire. 800 block of Newburn Avenue. Warehouse fully involved. All nine regional fire departments have responded for a total of 35 firefighters actively fighting the blaze.
>
> Intense heat and thick smoke slowed firefighters trying to get to the source, depleting a good portion of the oxygen tanks before anyone could get close. The intensive heat caused the cement flooring to begin to crack and four firefighters were injured when a beam fell on them as they were evacuating all firefighting personnel.

Marine dialed Aunt Betsy's house. Chet answered.

"Chet, please tell Aunt Betsy that I really want to talk with her. I have a call I must go on. I'll try and chat with her tomorrow after I get in."

* * * * *

Aunt Betsy watched as Chet hung of the phone. "Well, Marine will not be making it after all. Another arson fire."

"Oh my. I had hoped we'd get to see her. I don't think she knows Drake's in town. You don't think that was whom she meant when she said my friend was in town. I hope she didn't run into him on the street. I wanted to tell her first."

"That would be a good thing to do. She did not sound upset when she said it; it was more matter of fact."

"These arson fires are really affecting a lot of people."

"Yes. There have been five fires in the last three nights with several victims. I am sure it is running Marine and the special unit ragged."

"All of them arson?"

"I do not know. When is Drake coming over here?"

Aunt Betsy walked over to the counter. "He said he'd drop by after eight this evening. It's about four thirty. He wanted to give me time to prepare Marine. Guess I don't have that to do."

"She did say she wanted to talk with you. Marine said she would see you after she gets in from work, probably tomorrow morning sometime. I imagine they will pull another all-nighter."

"You know, I think I'll go to Belle's in the morning and pick up several blueberry muffins. They are delicious. They put the large sugar crystals on top. Marine loves those warmed with butter inside and a piping hot cup of coffee. You should drop by and join us. I bet she'd enjoy seeing you, too."

"I might do that. What time do you think?"

"Oh, I don't know. I'll go by Belle's early. Let's say you drop by here around nine. I should be back by then. Besides, depending on when she gets home, Marine will at least want to get a little rest."

"Well, sounds good to me. I will head on home since she will not be making it by tonight." Chet got up and kissed Aunt Betsy on the cheek. "I will see you in the morning."

"Thanks for talking with me today. And, thanks for hosting Drake."

"He is not a bad roommate. I never know when he leaves, and I do not know when he comes in. He is almost too quiet."

"That's the MI6 training. I had it, too, you know."

"You have to tell me that story sometime. You can add it to the others you still need to tell me." Chet smiled. "Marine said she was surprised by what she had learned about your life. I guess I have not been a very good psychiatrist since I have not asked you much about your past."

"You did what I wanted you to do. You have been here for me and loved me. I've loved you. That's all we need."

Chet waved goodbye and closed the kitchen door behind him. Aunt Betsy got up, walked over to her hiding place, and checked her gun. It wasn't Drake that Marine was signaling me about. She saw Aunt Jeannie. She looked down at her gun. You're sleeping in the pocket of my nightgown tonight.

FIFTEEN

....

NO REST FOR THE WICKED

The morning sun was starting to break through the early fog. Aunt Betsy placed her gun into her purse and walked out to her car. If I see Aunt Jeannie, I'll just have to take care of business. She backed out of her driveway and drove to Belle's.

"Well, good morning, Aunt Betsy!" Belle called as Aunt Betsy walked through the door. Belle walked over to her and gave her a big hug. "I haven't seen you out on an early morning in a long time. What can I do for you?"

"I'd like some of your lovely blueberry muffins. I'll need a half-dozen. I'm taking them home for Marine and Chet to enjoy."

"They are due to come out of the oven in about ten minutes. You sit over there. I'll bring you some coffee."

"Oh, good. Freshly made is even better." Aunt Betsy walked over to the table where Belle pointed. She looked around the restaurant. Sitting at the back table were Fish, Doc, Roy, LT, and a few of the other firefighters from Marine's old station. She walked over to them.

"Hello, guys. How are you?"

"We're beat, Aunt Betsy," Roy said.

"Yes, we are. We've been on a fire call all night," Fish said. "That Letsco sure has her hands full with all of these arsons. We've been doing a good job putting them out. It's her job to find the culprit."

"Wow," LT said. "I didn't think you knew those big words, Fish. We're all proud of you."

"I wanted to say 'A-hole,' but with Ms. Lanter standing there, I don't think I should."

"Don't mind me, Fish," Aunt Betsy said as she patted him on the back. "I hope I get to see Marine later. She said she wanted to come by for a visit. Did you say she was back at her office or do you guys know?"

"She was still at the fire scene when I packed up the last of our tools," Doc said. "That was about an hour ago. Good seeing you, Ms. Lanter."

"Oh, Doc. Haven't you retired?"

"I have three more weeks. I'm counting the days now."

"I can imagine." Aunt Betsy saw Belle come out with her bag of muffins. "I better head over and pay the bill. You fellas have a safe day."

"You, too, Ms. Lanter. See ya," Fish called. The others all said their goodbyes.

Aunt Betsy walked over to Belle. "How much do I owe you?"

"They're on the house. I know Marine has worked hard. Let's call it my contribution to her and the fellas work. You never got your coffee."

"Now, Belle. You'll never stay in business if you keep this up. It's okay about the coffee."

"I'm doing fine, Aunt Betsy. You have a good visit with Marine and tell her to drop in. I haven't seen her for a while."

"I'll do that. Thanks again—" Aunt Jeannie walked through the door just as Aunt Betsy was turning to leave.

"Well, look what kind of people they serve in this joint." Aunt Jeannie said with a sneer. She walked up close to Aunt Betsy and nudged her in the shoulder. "Can't you see where you're going?"

Aunt Betsy flung her arm back and said, "You don't want to start nothing in here. Now, step out of my way."

Aunt Jeannie threw a punch that hit Aunt Betsy squarely on the jaw causing her to stagger back, drop her purse, and fall across a chair.

"Just as I thought, you've lost your touch."

Aunt Betsy got back on her feet and threw the muffins at Aunt Jeannie. She saw the men get up out of their chairs, and she motioned to them to stay back. She grabbed a cup of coffee sitting on a nearby table and threw it at her, too. While Aunt Jeannie was dodging trying to avoid the coffee cup, Aunt Betsy reached for her purse. Aunt Jeannie stepped on the strap just as Aunt Betsy was about to retrieve it.

"Oh, no you don't," Aunt Jeannie said.

"Oh, yes, I will." Aunt Betsy managed to jerk the purse up and away. At the same time, she maneuvered herself around to the back of Aunt Jeannie and clipped her in the back of the knee, knocking her down. Aunt Betsy then took a bowl of oatmeal that was sitting on a table and dumped it on Aunt Jeannie. She picked up a hot pot of coffee.

A Time for Fire

"Stop!" Drake called to Aunt Betsy. "You don't want to do that!"

"Sure, I do."

"Not here. Come on, Aunt Betsy. Ma'am," Drake said to Aunt Jeannie as though he didn't know who she was. "Are you okay?" He helped Aunt Jeannie up to her feet.

"Yes, son, I am." Aunt Jeannie said. "Thank you for helping me. That woman went crazy. She ought to be locked up."

"You started it," Aunt Betsy said. "Now, what are you going to do?"

"Ma'am," Drake said to Aunt Jeannie. "You should leave. I'll take care of getting the place cleaned up." He turned to Aunt Betsy. "You sit over here."

"I'll leave, but this isn't over," Aunt Jeannie said as she went out the door.

"Who was that woman? I'll never let her in here again. You really stood up for yourself. Man, what a fight!" Belle came over and brought Aunt Betsy a new bag of muffins. "Are you okay?"

"Yes. Just mad that she got the better of me. I should have shot her when I had the chance."

Belle started to laugh. "You sure have a feisty streak about you."

Fish, Roy, and the other guys were standing nearby. "You can come over now, boys. Thanks for offering to help."

"We would have stepped in, but you made it clear we were to stay back. We knew to listen to you." Fish said as he handed her purse to her. "Feels kind of heavy. What are you packing?"

"Yeah. And, where did you learn to fight like that? We had no idea you had it in you," Roy said as he sat down beside Aunt Betsy.

"My thirty-eight, and I should have used it."

They all laughed. Aunt Betsy looked at Drake as he stood there watching her.

* * * * *

Charles Massie had been working in the evidence room most of the night. The last five fires had been so close together, he hadn't gotten all of his paperwork caught up. He stepped out long enough to go to the bathroom and to grab himself another cup of coffee. *If I'm lucky, I'll be out of here by ten. The sun's up and I'm exhausted.* As he made the turn to go down the corridor, he noticed that the evidence door was ajar. He slowly opened the door wider.

A Time for Fire

"What are you doing in here, Matt?" Charles walked in and over toward Matt.

Matt turned quickly, hit Charles in the head, and knocked him to the ground. He went out the door. Charles got up and went after him. As he turned the corridor, he saw Matt running down the hall.

"Wait! Matt! Come back here. What's wrong with you? Matt!"

Charles saw Matt run through the office, out into the parking lot, and get into a truck. He noticed that the truck was not the vehicle Matt always drove. This truck was banged up and had rust spots. As Matt started to pull out of the parking spot, Charles ran toward him and got in front of the truck.

"Stop, Matt! Stop!" Charles looked at Matt and realized he looked different. Matt appeared to be smiling at him. Matt wouldn't do that, Charles thought to himself. Matt rarely smiled. The truck kept coming toward him. Charles was too slow in getting completely out of the way and was hit by the front bumper of the truck. The truck sped out of the parking lot.

Charles fell hard, hitting his head on the pavement.

Marine and Tom happened to be coming into the parking lot when they saw the commotion and the driver race the truck out of the parking lot. Marine stopped the car and they both rushed over to Charles. His head gushed blood. He looked up at them with a look of shock.

Within five minutes, the paramedics arrived and put him on the gurney.

"Double," Charles managed to say before he went unconscious.

"What did he mean?" Tom asked as the paramedics loaded Charles into the ambulance.

"I'm not sure. We need to go see what he was working on. And, was that Matt we saw driving or someone that looked like him?"

"That's a good question."

It took them thirty minutes for Marine and Tom to go through the notes Charles had on his desk. Nothing pointed to anything unusual. Marine had begun to gather together some papers and had already secured the video from the surveillance of the parking lot. The last twenty minutes of the video had the scenes of when Charles was hit.

"I just got off the phone with the Chief," Tom said as he walked over to their desk area.

A Time for Fire

"He's at the hospital and said that Charles was in ICU. He's in a coma. Evidently, he hit his head pretty hard. That was scary watching that truck go after him. I wonder what Charles meant when he said 'double'?"

"I've been thinking about the guy driving the truck. Did you get a good look at him? I know I got a glimpse. He looked like Matt, but thinner."

"I don't think I got any better look at him than you did. He did favor Matt. But, Matt doesn't drive a truck. He has a sedan."

"Do you think Charles was trying to tell us that the guy was Matt's double? His brother, Pat?"

"How can that be? Pat is dead. Isn't he?"

"Now, that is a good question. I'm going to take this video of the scene in the parking lot and have Archie and his guys at the tech lab see if they can enhance some stills I've noted with a time stamp. Maybe they can determine who the driver of the truck might be." Marine paused and thought for a moment. "Also, I need to visit Aunt Betsy. I'll be back in a few hours."

"I told the Chief I'd head over to relieve him at the hospital. He wants someone to stay with

Charles. It's a shame he doesn't have family close by. The Chief said his wife and son should be here later this evening. Call my cell if the guys turn up anything."

"Will do. First, we've got to get a handle on this arsonist. I have a feeling it's going to get wicked around here if we don't."

"Yeah. I think it already has."

* * * * *

Marine dropped off the video. Archie told her it would take a few hours. They were in the middle of working on a video taken during the investigation of the scene of the latest arson fire. They would finish it and get to her video right away.

Marine was sure that who she saw was Pat. She just knew it. She couldn't prove it, yet. While she was walking back to her Durango, she caught a glimpse of a figure. She decided to double back to cut around the building. As she walked into the alley, she felt a gun pointed into her back.

"Steady. I'm a little trigger happy today."

"Aunt Jeannie," Marine said as she turned to face her. "What a way to greet me after all we've been through? When did you come to town?"

"You can stop right there. I taught you all of your tricks. Put your hands on your head. I have no plans of getting into it with you here and now. That will happen later. I wanted my chance to tell you things you need to know—to straighten out the lies you've been told about me."

"What lies? I wasn't aware anyone has lied."

"Funny. That Betsy you call Aunt is not at all who you think she is. She is more diabolical than you could imagine."

"Speaking of funny, she says the same thing about you. I wonder whom I should believe. Let's see, the woman who tried to have me killed by Ana-Geliza or the woman that has taken me in, given me a home, and had no idea who I was?"

Aunt Jeannie let out a hysterical laugh.

"Careful, Aunt Jeannie. You may draw attention."

"Shut up. You know nothing. Aunt Betsy knew you before. She knew you in ways you have no idea. Who do you think brought you to me? Don't you get it, Marine? You are about as dense as you always were."

"Dense? You always said I was your brightest. So, now I'm dense. Why? Because I choose not to believe you? What do you mean that Aunt Betsy brought me to you?"

"She brought you to me to raise you as she wanted you to be. She took you away from your parents. They were killed because of Aunt Betsy. She had me turn you into a killing machine, like she is, like we both are. I did to you what was done to us."

"You are crazy. My parents died in a car crash. I was lost, in an orphanage for three years before you came and got me. I might have lost my memory when you sicced Ana-Geliza on me, but I since have it back. Why do you hate me so? I've always tried to do as you asked."

"You left me."

"Yes. I left because I didn't know whom I was. Why kill me over that?"

"You left before. Ana-Geliza told me you were leaving when you went to the Caribbean. She said you wouldn't be coming back."

"What? I had no intentions of leaving then. I only left after the cruise because I had no idea who I was. I was offered a place to live. Besides, how would Ana-Geliza know what I was planning? I barely knew her. I never saw her before the cruise ship." Marine was beginning

A Time for Fire

to understand that Aunt Jeannie was crazy and was determined to do her harm. She maneuvered herself around to where her back was up against the wall. She knew it would give her a strategic leverage when she made her move.

"She knew you! She was my daughter! She worshipped you!"

"What? Your daughter?"

"Yes. You're more of a fool than I took you for. She was that little girl that always hung around you when you were in training."

"There were several little girls. I never noticed her." Marine watched Aunt Jeannie blink and noticed her speed was slow. Aunt Jeannie had also moved past her safety zone. Marine knew that if she could catch her looking down, she'd have a chance.

Aunt Jeannie had become solemn. "No one ever noticed my Ana-Geliza. She was so beautiful." She looked down. Like a flash, Marine disarmed Aunt Jeannie and turned the gun on her.

"Well, she's dead now."

"And, your grandmother will be! When Aunt Betsy killed Ana-Geliza, I planned to do her in and you, too!"

Marine stopped mid-stride. She had the gun pointed at Aunt Jeannie. "What?"

"Such a blooming fool. Don't you get it? Aunt Betsy is your grandmother!"

Marine pulled the gun up and pointed it at Aunt Jeannie's forehead. "Explain yourself."

"You two are just alike. You will never change. Aunt Betsy tried that same stupid trick with me in the restaurant the other night. Oh, she managed to knock me down, but she didn't kill me. And, you know what?" Marine nodded for her to continue. "You won't either."

"What makes you think that?"

"You won't shoot me if you want to see your precious Wayne and Aunt Betsy again."

"Why? Where are they?"

Aunt Jeannie backed away and said, "You'll have to find them to find out where they are."

Marine took aim. If she shoots, what happens to Wayne and Aunt Betsy? She ran the possibilities. She may have them. She lowered her gun.

"Damn."

*****

As Marine drove, as though she was going to a fire, to find Wayne, she thought about her encounter with Aunt Jeannie. She wasn't sure who was crazier—the arsonist or Aunt Jeannie. She said Aunt Betsy was my grandmother. Jeez. I would have thought Aunt Betsy would have told me. Wouldn't she?

Marine walked into Wayne's office. "Is he in?"

The receptionist nodded affirmative. "May I ask who you are?"

"Marine Letsco, Fire Investigator."

"And, it is in regards to?"

"To a slew of arson fires. May I see him?"

"Not right now. He's in a meeting. You can take a seat. He should be available soon."

Marine took a seat near the door. She was glad to know he was in his office and Aunt Jeannie hadn't kidnapped him. She was bluffing. Marine thought about Aunt Betsy. She picked up her cell phone to dial her to see that she was okay.

"Ma'am," the receptionist pointed up to a sign. It read 'No Cell Phone Use!'

"Great," Marine said as she slammed her phone down. She thought about texting, Aunt Betsy but decided she'd text Chet instead. Maybe he could check on Aunt Betsy for her, and not cause her alarm. Then, she read the sign again. At the bottom, it said, 'this includes no texting.'

Just then, a door opened, Wayne and several other fire department personnel filed out. "I'll be in touch with you on the progress." The gentlemen walked out and Wayne turned to Marine. "This is a surprise. I don't think you've been here since we moved to our new offices. Come on in, what's up?"

"Wayne." He looked back and motioned to the receptionist. "Uh, Chief Foglesong, I need to speak with you." Wayne closed the door behind Marine.

"Sorry about that. I know we don't have anything to fear about being in the same department, but I don't want to provide gossip for anyone. Now, what's up?" He motioned for her to sit beside him on his office couch.

Marine smiled. "I've got something I need to tell you."

Marine began to explain to him about Aunt Jeannie, what she learned from her about Ana-Geliza's death, as well as her threats to harm him and Aunt Betsy. Marine confided that she was having a hard time dealing with the news that Aunt Betsy might be her grandmother.

"Wayne, I just don't know what to believe. I'm scared. If Aunt Jeannie told the truth, what then? Why hasn't Aunt Betsy told me? Why keep it secret? And, does Chet know?"

Wayne placed his arm around Marine's shoulder. "You know you have just dumped a lot of information in my lap. I'm still thinking about what you said regarding this Aunt Jeannie person. You say she taught you how to be an assassin? And, she and Aunt Betsy used to be friends?"

"Yes. It is all so messed up."

"You can say that again. Have you talked with Aunt Betsy?"

"No. I was going to go see her next. I was going to call her and warn her about Aunt Jeannie. I came here first to make sure you were all right. What am I going to do?"

"You're going to do like you always do. You're going to take a deep breath and move forward. You've been dealing with a lot of stress from working on all these arson cases. And now this. You have it in you. You've proven that already. You need to believe in what you can do. I'm a big boy. I can take care of a little old woman. And, I have a feeling your

Aunt Betsy, or your grandmother," Wayne smiled, "can take care of herself, too."

"I guess you're right. I'm glad you're okay."

"Yes. And, I bet if you call Aunt Betsy, you'll find out that she is okay, too."

"May I call her now?"

"Sure. Use my desk. I'll step out and give you some privacy."

Marine picked up the phone; Wayne threw her a kiss before he opened the door.

Aunt Betsy's phone rang and rang. There was no answer. I don't like this feeling I'm having. Marine walked out into the reception area. Wayne was nowhere in sight.

"Tell Wayne, I mean, Chief Foglesong I'll call him later."

SIXTEEN

MORE WICKEDNESS

When Wayne came back to his office there was a note on his door from his receptionist. The message said that Marine would call him later. With all of her difficult challenges, he found he was starting to like her more than a little bit. They had fun together and he hoped he could get her to settle down in New Brook. The revelation of Aunt Betsy being Marine's grandmother troubled him. He wondered what Chet knew about it all.

After he finished some paperwork, it was about six o'clock when he shut off his office lights and walked down to the front door. He waved good night to the security guard. Walking to the parking lot, he saw a cream-colored sedan parked beside his dark black

Durango. As he walked up to his vehicle, a nice looking elderly lady got out of the sedan.

"Sir?"

"Yes, ma'am?"

"Could you help me? It seems my car keys are stuck in the ignition switch. I can't get the car to turn over."

Wayne noticed that the woman looked as if she was dressed for church, with a hat, gloves, and a fine detailed wool coat. But, instead of a skirt, she had on slacks. "Sure, let me see what I can do." He walked over to her driver side door, and she followed close behind him. He started to turn back to say something.

"You can go ahead and sit down if you like. It will be easier."

"Oh, okay." Wayne slipped into the driver's seat. Suddenly, he felt a severe electrical shock. He began to writhe in pain. Then, he felt a needle stick in his arm. All sounds faded into darkness.

* * * * *

Aunt Jeannie maneuvered Wayne to the other side of the seat. She wire-tied his hands and feet.

A Time for Fire

She then took off her church hat, shed the coat, and put on a baseball cap.

"Let's go join Aunt Betsy. That Seconal should keep you down for a while."

SEVENTEEN

PUTTING THE PUZZLE TOGETHER

Before Marine could make it out to Trout House Falls to check on Aunt Betsy, she received a phone call that Charles had come out of the coma. She looked at her watch. It was about five o'clock. She hated she did not get to say goodbye to Wayne. She would have to call him later. She headed for the hospital. Maybe Charles could help them figure out what was going on with Matt.

When Marine got to Charles' room, the only person there was a guard at his door. She showed her badge and he motioned for her to go in. Charles was sitting up in his bed, eating gelatin.

"I bet you are glad to be out of ICU."

"Yep. But, you know, I never knew I was there until the doctor told me. I woke up in here."

"You don't look too bad after all you've been through. Can you tell me anything about it?"

"Sure. Have a seat. Would you like something to eat or drink? I'll call a nurse and have something ordered." Charles smiled. Marine thought it was good he had his sense of humor.

"I'll listen while you tell me what you remember."

"Oh, I remember it all. The doctor said I was lucky. The accident didn't do any damage to my brain."

"Good. So, what happened?"

Charles shared how he found Matt in the evidence room and how he chased him out into the parking lot.

"Then the strangest thing happened," Charles said as he shook his head. "Matt didn't look like Matt as that truck came barreling at me. I was frozen in my spot. It had to be Pat! And, you know what? I thought I was seeing a ghost 'cause we all knew Pat was declared dead."

A Time for Fire

"That's why you said 'double' just before you passed out?"

"I did? I don't remember that part."

"Well, you did. You believe it was Pat and not Matt?"

"Yes. I do. He was too thin to be Matt. Besides, he wasn't driving Matt's car and his clothes looked like crap."

"Okay. Anything else?"

"Yeah. When he was in the offices, he was hanging around the evidence room a lot. He didn't eat all the sweets he used to eat. I bet Tom hadn't noticed because you both have been so busy with these arson fires. But, now that I have time to think about it, it wasn't Matt who we've been seeing for several weeks now."

Marine nodded her head. "It's good to hear that you think Pat has been acting like Matt. I've had my suspicions for a while, too."

"Yes. And I'll you something else. I think he's been planting the puzzle pieces in our evidence boxes."

"What makes you think that?"

Charles reached over to his things that were setting on the side table. "Because I managed to pick this up as he was running down the hall. He must have dropped it. You'll notice it doesn't have any glue on it. Like he was preparing to put it together and use it."

Marine studied the puzzle piece. She had looked at the other pieces so much she could just about tell where to place this particular piece in the puzzle. "I believe you're right, Charles. Good detective work. You get some rest and hurry up and get well. Tom and I will get Pat for what he has done to you. I'll be back to see you real soon."

"Thanks, Marine. I'm glad I could help."

* * * * *

Marine reached for her cell as she was about to get into her Durango. "This is Marine."

"Hi, Marine. It's Drake." Marine paused. *What the hell is he calling me about?*

"Hi, Drake. Are you calling from London?"

"No. I'm in town."

"Oh. When did you arrive?"

"Marine, where are you?"

"Why? Is something wrong?"

"Maybe. I talked with Chet a bit ago. He can't find Aunt Betsy."

"What?"

"Have you talked with her?"

A Time for Fire

"No. I talked with Wayne earlier after I had an unexpected encounter with Aunt Jeannie—"

"When did you see her?"

"Jeez, Drake, give me a chance." Marine closed her truck door and started the engine. She backed out of her parking space and pulled out of the lot. "About an hour. No, wait. More like an hour and half ago now. I—"

"Damn. I wish I'd known."

"Christ, Drake. Slow up. I didn't even know you were in town. I tried calling Aunt Betsy. There was no answer. I was going to call Chet when I got the call to go to the hospital. What do you want from me?"

"Sorry. I'm worried. Why were you at the hospital?"

"Long story. One of our colleagues was run over by a suspected arsonist. Anyway, let me see where Wayne is. Aunt Betsy has been going off on her own a lot these last few days. I'll call you back. Wait! Where are you?"

"I'm at Trout House Falls."

"Okay. I'll head that way. I wanted to talk with Chet and Aunt Betsy anyway. Is Chet with you?"

"He's on his way. He just finished seeing his last patient."

"I'll be there in about fifteen or so minutes." Marine hung up her cell, pulled the Durango over to the side of the road, and dialed Wayne.

Wayne's office phone rang and went to voice mail. Marine left a message, and then called his cell phone. It went to voicemail. Just then, her cell phone rang. It was Wayne calling her.

"Hello, Wayne?"

"No, little Marine. Wayne can't talk right now. He and your Grandmother Betsy are tied up."

"Aunt Jeannie, wait. Don't hang up!" The phone went dead.

Marine called Drake back.

"Marine, where are you?"

"Listen. Aunt Jeannie just called me using Wayne's cell phone. Get a trace on it and use the GPS quick. She may have already disarmed it. But, wait a minute. I have another call coming in." Marine switched calls.

"Yes, This is Letsco."

"Marine, Tom here. How close are you to getting to the office?"

"I'm not far. I was on my way home. I'll turn around. I just left Charles."

A Time for Fire

"Yes. I know. I called to check on him and he told me he'd talked with you. We got the video analysis back. It wasn't Matt. Archie and the lab techs believe it was Pat. They used their facial recognition software and they're about eighty percent sure. That means Matt is missing. We've got to find him if he isn't dead already."

"We will find him, Tom. I'll be there as soon as I can." She hung up Tom's call.

Damn. Marine pondered what to do. She had to save Matt. He would walk through fire for his colleagues. She switched her call back to Drake.

"Drake?"

"Yes. Chet is here now. Are you close?"

"I can't deal with Aunt Betsy and Wayne right now. It's a long story. I have to go find Matt, a colleague of mine. You have to find where Wayne and Aunt Betsy are being held. I should be able to connect with you as soon as we find Matt. Can you do that for me?"

"What?"

"Listen, Drake. I know Aunt Jeannie. She won't kill them until I'm there. I have time to deal with this other crisis. You just find out where she is holding them. I'll get to you as soon as I can. Okay?"

"Of course. I'll get things rolling on this end. You call or text me when you can join me and I'll update you on things."

Marine hung up the cell and drove straight to the office.

EIGHTEEN

....

COUNTING STARS

Tom met Marine as she came through the door. He began spouting off orders. He made it clear that he had a thousand questions and wanted all details. Marine tried to focus on Matt, but her mind kept wandering to Wayne and Aunt Betsy.

"Marine, are you listening?"

"Uh, yes. Sorry. What did you say again, Tom?"

"I asked what are we going to do? How will we ever figure out where Pat and Matt are located?"

"You need to relax. Now, think. We don't know that Pat is with Matt. Besides, we don't know for sure that it is Pat."

"Who else could it be? I mean, really."

"We have supposed proof that Pat is dead. Why should we doubt the police reports?"

"I know Matt. He wouldn't run Charles down. You told me that even Charles thinks it was Pat."

"Hey, guys! What you doing?" Fish said as he, Roy, and Doc came walking into their office. Fish patted Marine on the back. "We wanted to come thank you, both."

"Hi, fellas," Marine smiled. "For what?"

"You haven't heard?" Roy asked. "Chief Bottoms got axed."

"Oh, yes. We were hoping you'd tell us we'd done something else wonderful." Tom asked.

"Today. It was official. The big brass came to the station and booted him out. They said it was because of your work. We felt we had to come and thank you. You two have done a great service. We were thinking of murdering the SOB. You saved me and my retirement." Doc said as he took a seat. "Hey, what's this? You have free time you can work a puzzle?"

"You always were a quick study," Marine smiled at Doc. "I'm happy that Chief Bottoms is no longer a menace to the department. I'm sad it had to happen the way it did. You realize that

A Time for Fire

Tom and I had no choice." The guys nodded. She then explained about the puzzle pieces.

"So, you're saying this is a puzzle that has been used to reveal this 'Randle the Candle' arsonist?" Roy asked. "I mean, what kind of dad blame fool would do something like that?"

"You know," Fish said. "Look at this Doc. Does this look like a fire you remember fighting? I swear I think it looks like the old Simmon's Farm. You remember don't you, Roy?" The three stood up over the puzzle pieces and studied them. They moved a few pieces around.

"Did you notice these here?" Roy asked as he picked up the ones with lettering. "These have the photographer's signature on them. This was done by an old friend of mine, Tom Carlyon."

"Well, you're right, Roy. I remember him. He was always around taking photographs," Fish said.

"Yeah. He also had many of his pictures made into puzzles Come to think of it. I've got several in my house." Doc joined in. "I bet I have one of his other pictures of this fire. It was a special fire because kids had used the farm all the time for partying. We thought it was an arson fire, but we never could prove it."

"Come to think of it, we had a small arson fire back at that same location about three weeks ago, didn't we?" Fish said. "Sure, we did. Remember. Matt said he was assigned to investigate it. We ran into him about three days after the blaze."

"Really?" Tom stepped in. "Where did you see Matt?"

"Oh, we were at Belle's. He came in and said he was headed out to the Old Simmon's Farm to investigate the shed burning. Some of us thought it was accidental while others thought it was an arson fire set by kids playing or trying their hand at smoking. Matt said he hated that old place. He mentioned he had seen enough of it when he was a kid. I thought that was a funny thing to say." Roy picked up another puzzle piece and looked at it closely. "Did you see this here?" He handed the puzzle piece to Marine.

She studied it. "What do you see, Roy?"

"Look closely. It is a candle burning."

"Damn. We never saw that!"

"I imagine you have a lot to do now. We probably should leave before another tone

A Time for Fire

strikes. Thanks again, for all you did for us." Fish shook both their hands as did Roy and Doc. "We'll treat you both to dinner at Belle's some night."

The guys turned to leave. As they did, they passed Matt walking in.

"Man, Matt. You look crappy. Your clothes are awful ragged. What gives with you?"

"Shut the hell up," Matt said as he kept walking.

"What gives, Matt? That's not like you mouthing off." Fish started to grab the man he thought was Matt.

"Stop, Fish. He ain't worth it," Roy said as he held Fish back. Matt kept on walking into the office ignoring them.

"I don't ever remember Matt acting like that before," Doc said. The guys went on out.

Marine had observed the commotion.

Matt walked up to her and Tom acting innocent. "What was their beef?" he asked.

"They came to share some news. Speaking of news, Charles is out of ICU. Did you know he was in the hospital? His appendix burst." Tom said.

Matt looked surprised. "ICU? Really? When?"

"When what?" Marine said. "You know he was about killed today?"

Matt looked down at the desk and began to bend the corner of a sheet of paper acting as though he was trying to think. "Uh, no. I didn't."

Marine decided that she would test Matt to see if he was really himself. She walked over to the counter behind her desk and lifted out a small plate of fresh sweet rolls that Belle had made. She had asked Belle to deliver them to her office earlier that day.

"I got these earlier. I thought that maybe we'd enjoy them, especially if we had to work late tonight. Here, Matt. Try these." Marine handed the plate to Matt.

Matt nudged the plate away. "I've never liked them that much. They make my stomach hurt."

Marine and Tom looked at each other. Tom nodded his head. Marine knew by the look on his face that he agreed with her. This man standing before them was not Matt. He would have dived into eating those sweet rolls. This person had to be Pat after all. Marine noticed his reaction to Tom's body language. She saw him begin to make a move. He moved past

Marine, pushing her aside as he was making his way to run out the door.

Tom tripped Pat.

Marine and Tom jumped on Pat and they scuffled around the floor. After a few seconds, Marine managed to handcuff Pat. They picked him up, put him in a nearby chair, and started interrogating him about where Matt was located forgetting the protocol of reading him his rights.

"You do realize we could fingerprint him. We've got Matt's fingerprints on file," Tom said.

"That's all well and good, but we don't have time. We don't know where Matt is right now," Marine said as she held Pat in the seat. "Now, are you going to tell us where Matt is?" She nudged Pat leaning on him hard.

"I am Matt. Why don't you believe me?" Pat whined.

"You are no more Matt than I am." Tom walked around the room as he wrung his hands. "We're running out of time, aren't we?"

Pat laughed a hearty laugh. "You think you know so much. You have no idea. Randle the Candle has set fires his whole life and pretended to be many people. He has never been caught. I'm Matt, I'm telling you."

Marine, fed up with Pat's mouth, reached into her desk, and got a taser. "I'm going to light you up if you don't start talking."

Pat smiled. "You can't hurt me."

Marine stepped back a few feet and pressed the trigger. An electric charged fired across shooting two metal probe darts directly in the center of Pat's chest. He began to convulse and his body contorted as though he was in pain.

Marine let off the trigger.

"Yes. Yes, I'm Pat. But, I'll never tell you anything until you stop."

"Where's Matt?"

"I'm not telling ya."

Marine hit him again. Pat's body reacted by hopping off the chair and fell hard on the floor. Marine continued pulling the trigger longer. Pat shuddered, as he appeared to go into shock and acted semi-unconscious. While the taser was recharging, Pat began to come out of his stupor.

"You think that's going to do it?" Pat lifted his head, looked at her, and grinned.

Marine hit him again. Pat convulsed and started to slobber. She released the trigger.

A Time for Fire

"I'm asking you one more time, where is Matt?"

"Screw ya, I ain't telling ya. I hate him, I hate you, I hate me. You can torture me all you want, I ain't telling ya."

Tom walked over to Marine. "This isn't working."

"Sure, it is. We got him to confess he is Pat."

"What's going on here?" Chief Altizer said as he walked up. "Why do you have Matt handcuffed and tasing him? Have you lost your mind?"

Tom explained that Matt was Pat, and he had kidnapped Matt.

Marine looked down at Pat, "Where is Matt?"

Pat grinned and passed out.

"Damn. What will we do now?"

Marine walked over to the table with the puzzle pieces. Studied them and thought about what Fish and the guys said. She picked up the puzzle pieces with the writing on them. She looked up at Tom. "You know, Fish and the guys said Matt told them he'd had seen a lot of the Old Simmon's Farm when he was a kid. What if Pat had taken Matt there and they played? Maybe that is why Pat had this puzzle. I believe Matt's at this old barn."

"Okay. I get why you think that," Tom said. "But, how did Matt pull the assignment for the Simmon's fire the other day?"

"Pat rigged it. Just like he's been placing the puzzle pieces in the evidence boxes. He put the assignment on Matt's desk. Why not? Everyone here, including you and me, thought he was Matt."

"You may have something there, Letsco," Chief Altizer said. "I thought Pat was Matt, too."

"Since we believe Pat is 'Randle the Candle,' and we have no reason not to believe it, he would have set the fire out there the other day, saw to it that Matt was assigned, and that would have given him the perfect opportunity to kidnap Matt."

"Yes, but why?" Tom asked as he looked down at the puzzle. "Did he want to kill him?"

"He might have." Marine grabbed her keys and checked her gun. "Come on, we don't have any time to lose. Chief, would you call the paramedics and tell them to meet us out there? Matt might still be alive. Let's hope we get there in time."

A Time for Fire

* * * * *

An hour later, they had found Matt. He was severely dehydrated and needed medical attention. Pat had tortured him with cigarette butts and burned patterns on his chest. He was unconscious when the paramedics put him in the ambulance.

"Good job, Letsco and Willard," Chief Altizer said as he slapped the back of the ambulance. "I'll go to the hospital. You two deserve to go home and get some rest. You solved two important cases tonight."

"Thanks, Chief," Tom said.

Marine heard her cell phone ringing as she walked off to one side. She pulled it out of her pocket.

"Drake? Drake, can you hear me?" Marine heard Drake tell her he'd placed a device in her Durango that she'd left back at her office. He explained that it would track his throw away cell's signal. He would leave the cell in his car while he tracks down Aunt Jeannie. He told her, he'd call her when he had more to tell her.

Tom walked up. "What's going on?" Marine hung up her cell.

"I've got to go. An old enemy of mine has kidnapped Aunt Betsy and Wayne. You go home. A friend of mine is there and I'm going to meet him. Thanks for all you did and for believing in Matt."

"I can go with you."

"No, Tom. You can't. I used the taser on Pat. I'm already in a lot of trouble. You don't need to get your hands any dirtier. I know that someone will die tonight, and it won't be Aunt Betsy or Wayne. I'll see you tomorrow."

Marine turned, walked to her Durango, got in, and set her GPS to follow the signal sent by Drake's cell.

NINETEEN

WARRIORS

As Marine drove to meet Drake, she worried about Wayne and Aunt Betsy. She hadn't even had a chance to talk with Aunt Betsy about what Aunt Jeannie had told her. She hadn't spoken to Chet. Her time with Wayne flashed back through her memory. If only she had insisted, he stay with her. How did Aunt Jeannie kidnap them both?

She looked at the signal on her cell, and then at the GPS on the dash. It looked as though she had another few miles. Her cell rang.

"Where are you?"

"I'm about two or so miles out."

"When you get here, you know the drill. I'm about a mile into the woods from where you'll see my car. Remember, no lights."

Not long after hanging up, Marine pulled her car beside Drake's with her lights out. She eased out of her car, walked to the back, and quickly changed into her stealth black workout outfit that she always used on a reconnaissance job when she was working for TRANS. She liked using it when she worked out in the gym, so it was always with her. It felt strange being back on the job, so to speak. She hoped that they would be in time—that Wayne and Aunt Betsy were still alive.

It took her about ten minutes to make her way to Drake even with the moonlight lighting her path. She had taken her time, walking carefully, in order to not alarm anyone, especially Aunt Jeannie. She moved up beside Drake and crouched in behind a large groove of olive berry bushes that offered a good vantage point. The moonlight cast plenty of shadows, but Marine could make out the entrance to the old mine.

She tapped Drake on the shoulder and whispered, "Why do you think they are inside?"

Drake motioned he saw them go inside. Marine nodded she understood. Drake motioned he was ready for them to make their way on in.

A Time for Fire

The grass in front of the old mine was high, telling Marine that not many people had been walking around the area in a while. She looked at the jagged rock facings. The moonlight caused shadows to form that looked like jeering faces in the rocked surface. A rabbit scurried out from under a bush and along the path.

Drake stopped. Marine listened. The crickets continued to sing their chorus. Suddenly, they paused as a deep rumble of thunder could be heard nearby. Great, a rainstorm. Marine looked up and watched the moon being covered with the clouds rolling in. I want this over, she thought as she rubbed her hand over her face wiping away the sweat. It was humid and hot. A perfect summer night for someone to die.

Drake took the lead as they entered the mineshaft. They paused and listened for voices. No sound of humans but the crickets' chirping seemed to have escalated in anticipation of the pending storm falling upon them. As they walked steadily forward, Marine wondered if Aunt Jeannie had set up any traps. She felt she should have—whether I came in alone or not. She motioned to Drake to stop. He turned to look at her and just as he did, Marine saw a shovel come down on his head.

Marine jumped out of the way. Instinctively, she knew a bullet was heading toward her. She could hear the ricochet as it bounced off a rock above her head. Damn. That was close. She waited a minute or two before she moved her head out to look for Drake. All she could see was the dirt scuffed where he had fallen. Aunt Jeannie must have dragged him back with her.

"You might as well come on in. I only wanted to even the odds. He's not dead, but he'll have a horrible headache tomorrow."

Marine thought a moment and wondered if Drake was out cold or playing possum. She hoped possum was his idea of a good ploy.

"I'm coming in. Don't shoot."

"Why not?"

"Funny. You want this to be about you and me. So, why don't you let Wayne and Drake go? They haven't hurt you in any way."

"That's Drake? Well, I'll be damn. I had no idea Betsy had gotten him to come. Nice going there, Betsy. I should go ahead and shoot him."

"Wait. Why?"

Marine stepped forward into the light of the dimly lit room that Aunt Jeannie had set up.

A Time for Fire

Aunt Betsy and Wayne were seated at the back on wooden boxes. They both had tape on their mouths and their hands were tied behind their backs. Wayne's head looked like he had a gash where he must have hit his head at some point. He was obviously tired and probably dehydrated. Aunt Betsy looked less worn and angrier. She used her eyes to have me look to my right. I could see an arsenal of weapons and explosives. Aunt Jeannie wasn't planning to let any of us escape—not even herself. Drake and I had walked into a major trap.

"Because, you probably hit him hard enough he's already dead. Where's the fun in shooting a dead body? Besides, you want me. I'm here. Why waste time on him?" Marine walked around toward Wayne and Aunt Betsy as she talked.

Aunt Jeannie maintained her distance and adjusted her view as Marine circled to get herself next to them. This gave the added benefit of Drake being off to the side of Aunt Jeannie's full view. Marine was hoping he'd be able to make a move if he was still alive.

"Aren't you the sly one? And here I thought you were dense."

"I see you've added some charm to this old mine. Are you planning to remodel with the explosive touch?"

"Yes. You and your friends will have front row seats, too. And, it is about time we get started."

"I want something from you first."

"Gotten a little forward in your last minutes of life, have ya?"

"Maybe. Maybe not. I want you to tell Aunt Betsy, who Ana-Geliza was to you. I don't think she knew. I think she would have treated her differently if she had known." Marine hoped this would get Aunt Jeannie thinking about her daughter long enough to give Drake time to make his move. She was counting on it.

Aunt Jeannie walked over to Aunt Betsy and jerked the masking tape off her mouth. Aunt Betsy let out a small cry of pain, appearing to hold most of her reaction back.

"You killed Ana-Geliza, right?" Aunt Betsy nodded. "Why?"

"She was trying to kill Marine."

"What's Marine to you? Nothing. You threw away your only grandchild, and then had her parents killed. Ana-Geliza told me all about it and how Marine had killed her brother. Ana-Geliza was special. She was important to me."

"She was? Well, you should have taken better care of her." Aunt Jeannie turned to Aunt Betsy and was in the act of pulling her hand back to hit her.

"Aunt Jeannie, she didn't know," Marine said. Aunt Jeannie turned slightly and looked toward Marine, who stepped between Aunt Jeannie and Drake.

Aunt Jeannie turned back toward Aunt Betsy. "She was my daughter."

Aunt Betsy formed a smile on her face. "You don't say. Well, who would knock you up twice?"

As Aunt Jeannie pulled her gun around to point it at Aunt Betsy, Marine managed to drop down and roll along the dirt floor, coming up beside one of the guns sitting in the pile along the wall. She pulled the gun around, cocked it, and said, "Hold it, Aunt Jeannie."

Aunt Jeannie reached down, pulled Aunt Betsy up out of the seat, and positioned herself behind Aunt Betsy. "No. You hold it."

At the same time, Drake made his move removing his backup gun from his boot.

"I think we're in a stand-off," Marine said. "Set your gun down and we'll part friends."

Aunt Jeannie cackled a loud, wild laugh. "No, I don't think we are. All I have to do is shoot the fuse and we're all gone. Besides, what makes you think that gun is even loaded?"

"I know you, Aunt Jeannie. You taught us to always keep all guns loaded. Your mantra was 'Keep 'em Loaded or Die.' Remember?"

Marine smiled as she saw Drake wink at her, which was their signal to each other. "You've got a point there, Aunt Jeannie." Marine lowered her gun down.

"What are you doing, Marine?" Aunt Betsy asked.

Aunt Jeannie moved her gun from pointing at the explosives to pointing at Marine.

Drake shot.

Marine watched Aunt Jeannie slump to the ground.

* * * * *

By the time they got Wayne back to the hospital, he was unconscious. He'd lost a lot of blood and was severely dehydrated. Aunt Betsy was shaken up, but not hurt badly. The doctors wanted to keep her overnight, but she insisted on being released to go home. She was still in the examining room when the doctor told Marine that they were getting ready to move Wayne upstairs to ICU.

Drake walked up to Marine and handed her a cup of hot coffee. "It's made with one sugar and two creams, just the way you like it."

"You remembered. Thanks." She smiled. "What now?"

"They're working on Aunt Jeannie."

"Let's move into the hall." They walked through the curtained wall. "Did we have to save her?" Marine said as she took a sip. The hot liquid felt good going down.

"It was your call. I think INS, INR, and MI6 will be glad to have her off the streets."

"Yeah. I guess. It would have felt good finishing her off, though. All the lives she has harmed."

"You know that isn't what you want or believe."

"I guess. You know, Drake. Since all this started, I'm not sure who I am anymore, let alone what I want. At least before, I thought I was an orphan. I had a job to do. I did it. Now, where am I?"

"These last couple of years has been hard. I'm offering you security and love. I do love you, you know."

"Drake, I'm not sure what love is anymore. I know we've had great sex together, but I want more than that in my life. I have some unresolved things with Aunt Betsy or is it, Grandmother? Anyway, she and I need to talk. I'd like to make sure that Wayne is okay."

"I didn't mean you had to decide tonight. Will you consider coming with me?" Drake reached down and took Marine's hand. "We could have a good life."

"We could." Marine moved her hand from Drake's grasp and walked over to the window looking out over New Brook. "It's a beautiful night. Or is it morning already? I guess it's close." She looked at the clock on the wall and saw it was almost five thirty. "Drake, can you give me some time?"

"Yes. I won't be leaving here until Aunt Jeannie recuperates. How's nine in the morning? Seriously, can you meet then?"

Marine smiled. "Thanks, for being you. And for understanding." She patted Drake on the shoulder and walked toward Aunt Betsy's room.

A Time for Fire

As Marine turned the corner to the room, she saw Aunt Betsy getting back upon the bed.

"Code Black. Code Black. All points to Examining Room Two," the PA blared.

"That noise could wake the dead. Where have you been?" Marine said as she set her coffee cup down on the nightstand.

"I went to the bathroom."

"Did you, now? When can you leave?"

"The doctor said he was going to get my release papers. Are you taking me home?"

"No. I've asked Drake to do that. Chet is supposed to be at Trout House Falls to meet you. Aunt Betsy?" Aunt Betsy looked up at Marine. "This time, you will sleep upstairs in your house. I'll be home to sleep in my bed tonight." Aunt Betsy grinned. "And, one other thing. Don't think we're finished with this story Aunt Jeannie told me about you being my grandmother. You can plan on talking with me about it tomorrow. I want to be rested and sharp when you explain it."

Drake came walking into the room. "Well, it appears Aunt Jeannie had an aneurysm. That was her code black. She's dead."

"Well, wasn't that rude." Aunt Betsy chortled.

TWENTY

....

STEADY AS SHE GOES

The morning sun shone through the curtains as they flapped gently in the breeze. Marine rolled over on her side. She looked out at the view from her bed. The hills looked like they were rolling softly along. She could see several horses grazing in the field. It was a beautiful morning for July. She was ready to start over. To begin her new life. She hoped that those who knew her would understand her choices, and why she had made them. It had been a long time coming—a little more than two years since that fateful fall on the cruise ship. My life sure has taken some strange turns, she thought. And, now, I'm about to make another one.

Marine rose and stretched. It had been several weeks since she'd last slept through the night. It was good to not hear the fire paging tones go off on her cell. She loved being a fire investigator. It was productive. She felt she could do good work for her community and that made her feel proud of herself. Something she never really learned to do.

The cottage phone rang. Marine got up, picked up the receiver. "Yes?" She listened. "Okay, Chet. I'll be over in about forty or so minutes. I'm just now waking up. Yes. Yes, I was tired. Okay. I'll see you later. Tell Aunt Betsy I'll be over soon."

Marine hung up the phone, walked into the bathroom, and looked in the mirror. "You ready for this?"

* * * * *

Marine walked up the back steps. She wondered how long she would continue doing that simple act. She was about to make her decision based on how Aunt Betsy reacted to her while they talked. It was not going to be an easy time, but it had to be done. She took a deep breath and walked into the kitchen.

A Time for Fire

"Good morning, Aunt Betsy," Marine walked over to her at the counter. "How are you feeling this morning?"

Aunt Betsy smiled at Marine. "You're still speaking to me. That's something, I guess."

"Sure, I'm still speaking to you. How else will I learn what I need to know? Come on. Chet said you'd fixed a big breakfast. Let's sit down, eat, and enjoy our meal, then we can talk. What do you say?"

"I'd rather talk now."

"Would you? Really? I think those biscuits are calling to me." Aunt Betsy smiled.

Marine watched Aunt Betsy as she pulled a plate of biscuits that were warming in the oven out and set it on the table on an oven matt. "Here. Go ahead and fix you something to eat. I've made some cubed tenderloin medallions, fried up country style. There's some gravy here, too," she said as she placed the skillet with the tenderloin and a bowl of gravy on the table.

"Want me to get the jelly out of the fridge, or do I need to open a new jar?"

"You sit still. I got that together already, too. I have them here in my jam and jelly compote, some homemade orange marmalade, pear honey, and blackberry jam."

"Pear honey? Oh, my. What kind of bees makes that?"

"Human bees. It really isn't honey, as you'd think. It is made from fresh pears. A dear friend of mine, Mr. Nance, makes it. He gave me a jar this year. I have wanted to try it for some time. Now, mind you, it is sweet."

Marine began placing different samples of food on her plate. She started to get up again.

"Just where are you going?"

"I was going to get some coffee."

"Here you go. I got that prepared here in this pot, and here is a glass of milk for you, too. I know how you like to have both."

Marine began to enjoy each bite. "Aren't you going to sit and eat?"

Aunt Betsy came over and pulled her chair out, and set her coffee down. "Marine. I'm so very sorry." She started to cry.

Marine got up and put her arm around Aunt Betsy's shoulders. "Oh, Aunt Betsy. Don't—"

After a few minutes of hugging, they resumed eating and Marine and Aunt Betsy began to discuss the story of Aunt Jeannie. Aunt Betsy explained how she had a daughter, Edna, with a Japanese Tenant Farmer, George Takai Armstrong. They secretly married.

George was ambushed and murdered for what was thought to be fraternizing with 'white folk.' Marine listened intently without interrupting. Aunt Betsy continued and shared how Aunt Jeannie came to have custody of Marine.

Marine said, "Aunt Betsy, what is my real name? I have used so many aliases that I don't remember what it is."

"You have a gorgeous name. It is Marine Elizabeth Renee Henegar. We called you 'Marnie' for short."

"That's the name I remember, Marnie." Marine sat there entranced. She was going to learn about her family—especially her mother and father. Something she never thought she'd be able to do. The sun shining through the kitchen window was an omen. Things were looking brighter.

"Speaking of names, do you think you'd mind calling me Granny Bee?"

Marine stood back and looked at her. They both started laughing. Marine said, "More like 'Queen Bee.'"

Granny Bee explained how her second husband came into her life and provided a home for her and Edna, Marine's mother. Then, one day, she and Edna parted ways. Edna went off to Europe where she finished her education, met and married Marine's father, who was an English aristocrat's son. Marine's father, Jim Henegar, joined the diplomatic core. When Marine was three years old, her parents were stationed in France. Two years later, when they were killed in a boating accident, Marine was with her nanny at their home but wandered out of the house during the commotion of the nanny learning about Marine's parents. Marine was lost in the shuffle.

"It took me years to find you. I never gave up looking. I knew you were safe somewhere. I could feel it here," Granny Bee pointed to her heart.

Marine smiled. "Why didn't you keep me when you found me?"

"I wanted to. I wanted to very much. But, I had a dangerous job with INR. Jean was my friend. She had started a school for wayward girls right after the war. It seemed natural you would be safe there. Besides, I'd be able to keep tabs on you. You had lost your parents. I felt it cruel to come into your life, and then if something happened to me, you'd be all alone again. So, I chose this way. I know now that was wrong of me." Granny Bee began to cry again.

"That's why you gave me the cameo pin at Christmas? You knew all along?"

"Yes."

Marine got up, went upstairs, and then came back. She sat down at the table, took Granny Bee's hand. As she placed the brooch in her hand, she said, "Tell me about this."

Granny Bee began to cry. Marine waited with her arm on her shoulder. She said, "It was my mother's, wasn't it?"

"Yes."

"You wore it all the time after she died?"

"Yes."

"When I was little, you were the lady that I saw wearing this at Aunt Jeannie's place?"

"How did—"

"Oh, Granny Bee. I've searched for you my whole life. Why didn't you tell me?"

"I couldn't. Not with you being so fragile. Chet told me how your memory could come back. I didn't want to do anything that would harm that. So, I waited. Jean coming back into our lives was not something I expected or planned on. I thought we'd been lucky when Ana-Geliza seemed to have disappeared."

"Did you know she was Jean's daughter?"

"No. Not until she told me last night."

"Like you, I had no idea the security guard that was collateral damage in that explosion I did for TRANS was Ana-Geliza's brother."

"And, now we know it was also Jean's son," Aunt Betsy had a faraway look. She said, "I'm not ashamed of what I did. I had to protect you. That was all that mattered. My protecting you was all that mattered."

Marine reached over and hugged her. "You are my Granny Bee. Nothing will change that. Nothing."

* * * * *

When Marine walked out to her Durango, she realized she now had a family in New Brook, one she wanted to know more about. One that she wanted to be a part of and love back. She drove to the hospital where she hoped to learn that Wayne was okay. Drake said he'd meet her there.

Her cell rang. "Hello?" Marine listened. "Oh, okay Drake. I should be there in about another ten minutes or less. See you there."

Drake told her he had some last minute things to do with the paperwork on the death of Jean Velasquez also known as Aunt Jeannie and Jean Bathroy. She wondered if that part of her life was finally finished. She was ready to move on and have a happy life for a change.

After parking her Durango, she got out, and walked into the hospital, ready to tell Drake her news and to see how Wayne was doing.

* * * * *

Pat Pike would be long gone by the time another police officer found the jailer knocked out cold on the floor. The jailer didn't know what hit him. Pat Pike was free. He locked the jailer in his cell and ran.

* * * * *

"Good morning, Battalion Chief Wayne Foglesong. How are you feeling?" Wayne looked up as Marine walked in the door.

"I'm feeling better now that you are here. We've got to stop meeting like this." Marine walked over to the side of the bed, bent down, and kissed him. "Now, I know I'm going home."

"When do you get out of here?"

"The doc came by about an hour ago, said he would put in my paperwork. I was released."

"Why aren't you changing into your clothes?" Wayne smiled. "Oh, did they cut them off you last night?"

"Yes. My good khaki's too. I don't have any clothes here."

"I'll tell you what. I'll go to your apartment for you and get some clothes."

"No need," Chet said as he walked through the door carrying what Wayne would need to wear. "I dropped in to visit him while I was downstairs checking on a patient. So, I volunteered to help out." He laid the clothes at the foot of the bed.

"If you two want to go out into the hallway, I can change, and then I can get out of here faster than planned."

Marine and Chet walked out into the hallway.

"Have you talked with Aunt Betsy?" Chet asked.

"Yes. Have you?"

"No. Do I need to?"

"She can give you all of the details. But suffice it to say, she's not my aunt anymore. She's my grandmother."

Chet's mouth dropped open. Then, he rubbed his chin. "What?"

A Time for Fire

"Yep. You have a lot of catching up to do. You might want to plan to take the day off and talk with Granny Bee. That's what I call her now. It will help you understand things if you hear it from her. There are parts I'm not sure I understand."

"I cannot believe I have lived in the middle of all of this and had no idea what was going on." Chet shook his head.

Marine smiled as Wayne came out of his room still tethered to the IV tubing, stretching it as far as it would go.

"I don't think you're supposed to be out of bed officially yet, are you?"

"No, he's not," said the nurse walking up the hall. Wayne turned and went back into his room.

"Marine. I will go see Aunt Betsy or Granny Bee. I will check with you later, okay?"

"Sure, Chet. You're going to have an interesting day."

Chet waved and stopped to speak with Drake, who was walking down the hallway. *Now, I have to break the news to these two. One will not be happy. The other will not be sad.*

Wayne walked out of his room, this time the IV had been removed. "I'm free!"

"Yes. It looks like you are," Drake said and extended his hand to shake Wayne's. "Glad to see you up and about and feeling better. You looked pretty ragged last night."

"I don't mind telling you, I felt it, too. How I don't have a concussion is anybody's guess. That Jean lady hit me rather hard. Marine, you're going to have to explain this all to me. I know you've tried, but this time, I think I have an idea of how mean this woman can be."

"She's no worry for you anymore."

"Oh? You're taking her back to England with you?"

"No. Not as you think. She died last night. An aneurysm. So, she's out of all of our hair."

"Aren't we lucky?" Wayne smiled. "Thank you for all you did to save me and Aunt Betsy. What will you do now?"

"I just finished with my paperwork and will take Aunt Jeannie's body back to England with me. And, I've come to find out Marine's decision. Has she told you?"

Marine looked worried that Drake would blurt it out.

"Told me what?"

"I asked her to go back to England with me. She could work at MI6. When I shared with headquarters how she brought down Jean Velasquez, alias Aunt Jeannie, they were interested in hiring her right away. Besides, I'd like to establish more than a working relationship with this woman. You know what I mean?"

"Yes. I do believe I do," Wayne said. "So, what's your decision?" He turned to Marine for her answer.

"Wayne, this was hard for me to do. I just learned about Aunt Betsy being my grandmother. She and I had a nice long talk this morning."

"Okay. And?"

"Do you have any idea what you two are asking of me?"

"Yes, we do. Now choose!" Wayne placed his hands on his hips and took a determined stance.

"Drake, I'm sorry. I have to stay here. Do you understand?"

"I'm not surprised. It is tough competing against a family and a handsome guy like this one. I know when to cut my losses and leave." He walked over to Marine, gave her a long, loving kiss. "I'm glad I could be there for you. And, if you ever need anything—"

"I know." Marine hugged him one more time. Drake turned and walked away.

"You mean it? You really are staying here, with me?"

"Yes, Wayne, I'm staying. I've changed. My life is here now. I can become the person I've always wanted to be. I can help keep our community safe."

"This makes me happier than I can say. I'll be yours forever, you know that don't you?" Wayne leaned over and they shared a passionate kiss. "You mean so much to me."

"We can talk about this more, or kiss about it more later. Now, you go in there and finish your paperwork. I'll go down and get the car. I'm on the side parking lot area, so when you come out, I'll be right there and can help you get into the Durango."

"I won't need any help. You think I'm hurt or something, don't you? That woman couldn't hurt me. Not with you around." Wayne kissed Marine on the cheek. "I'll see you in a bit."

* * * * *

A Time for Fire

Marine saw Wayne being rolled out of the hospital wing. He got out of the wheelchair, stood up, and she waved to him. He began to walk toward her when Pat Pike jumped out from behind a nearby car and grabbed Wayne putting a gun to his head. Before she knew what had happened, Marine had her gun out and moved quickly toward them.

"Pat, you don't have any quarrels with this man. It's me you want. Let him go."

"No, ma'am. Ms. Marine, no, ma'am! He's mine. The last time I listened to you, I got put in jail. But, you forgot something real important. You forgot I had on Matt's clothes. He kept a handcuff key stashed in his belt. I knew it. I used it. Now, Ms. Marine. You get to deal with me. Right here. Right now."

"You need to listen to me, Pat. You need to let Wayne go. I'm not fooling." Marine positioned herself in a weaver stance and took aim.

Pat looked around. "There ain't n'body around. What ya gonna do, shoot me?"

In a calm, cool voice, with a touch of pleasure, she replied, "Yes."

You have just finished reading The Marine Letsco Trilogy.

Thank you! It is hoped you will share with your friends, tell your neighbors, and speak volumes about it on Amazon, Facebook, and Goodreads.

If you'd like to read more of Pam's stories

VISIT

PAM B. NEWBERRY

at her website:

http://pambnewberry.com

Become a **Happy V. I. P. Reader** (Very Important to Pam), read excerpts from her books, and learn more about the author.

WHAT ABOUT...?

The following are a few of the questions readers have asked:

1. **How did Aunt Betsy meet Aunt Jeannie?**

   Through working at the INR (Bureau of Intelligence and Research). They were office mates and became friends as a result.

2. **Why do they call each other Aunt?**

   It started out as a little joke between them after working on a case together. It stuck. Then, their family and friends began calling each of them Aunt. Aunt Jeannie never really liked being called by that name.

3. **What was Aunt Jeannie's son's (Ana-Geliza's brother) name?**

   That's something that may be revealed in a future series of books.

4. **Why did Aunt Jeannie turn evil?**

   She was evil from the start. It was below the surface, hidden. When she left INR, she met a man, who treated her badly. It resulted in her hating the world and all those around her. As a result, she allowed the evil lurking to surface, but with guarded caution. She was a tortured soul who thrived on torturing others for the joy of seeing others suffer because she had. Yet, she kept it hidden, which made her diabolical.

5. **Why did it take Marine so long to leave and begin to live a new life away from Aunt Jeannie?**

   Initially, Marine was blind to the evil in her life and the deeds she did in the name of her job. She thought she loved Aunt Jeannie. And, she liked the money, the life style. Marine didn't see a way out to where she'd be able to keep what she felt she needed. The loss of her memory helped her to make a significant change, and to realize what she thought she needed wasn't what she needed in the end.

6. **Who is Chet? What is in store for him in the future?**

   Now, isn't Chet an interesting guy? I mean, he is so funny. He never talks in contractions. He said that it made him feel like he wasn't completing his thoughts. And, he has a secret life. It would be fun to see what else he has to say. Wouldn't it?

7. **Will we ever see Aunt Betsy and Chet again?**

   I'd like to think so. There's so much about both of those characters that would be fun to explore; don't you think?

8. **What happens next for Marine?**

   That is a great question. Stay tuned. I'm sure Marine will surface again. Especially, if readers want her to come back. Who knows, it might even be in a different genre.

AN INTERVIEW WITH PAM

- **What will you do next, now that you have finished your first series?**

  I'm beginning work on a new series. Well, it's not actually 'new' to me, but it is a story I've revisited off and on over the last ten years.

- **What is it about?**

  It is a fantasy story with a touch of magic and romance. There will be the usual goblins, witches, and evil folk, but it will also have some interesting nuances to it, which I hope my readers will find enjoyable.

- **You've written a memoir and a thriller-suspense series, what makes you think you can write a fantasy story?**

  Magic! I didn't know I could write a memoir or even the thriller series. I'm learning, and I hope growing as a writer. My readers are giving me wonderful feedback, so I want to explore and continue this journey. I've dreamed about being a writer my entire life. It seems fitting to make a step forward into a new genre to learn more about the world of storytelling.

- **Will you ever revisit Marine and her story again?**

    Most likely. There are stories brewing and questions that have been left unanswered. Take Chet for example, who knows what kinds of adventures await him.

- **Who was your favorite character in the Marine Letsco Trilogy?**

    Oh my, there are so many. I actually liked them all, even the ones I killed off. Who was your favorite?

- **I'm asking the questions here (Pam laughs). When will your next series be published?**

    That's a good question. I ask readers to check back with me on my website. Become a Happy V. I. P. Reader, which is a Very Important Person to me. You'll get sneak peaks and advance information on my writing progress. The journey has just begun and I'm enjoying the ride!

ACKNOWLEDGEMENTS

The completion of a lifelong dream is not always an easy thing to share. But, for you, my devoted readers, who have stuck with me throughout my journey, I extend much thanks and wishes of eternal happiness to you. You have made it possible. Your steadfast encouragement, your devotion to following Marine's story, and your desire to connect with me have all been key to giving me the courage and aspiration to use my pen and produce my stories.

There are those people in the world who are critical to the successful completion of any goal. For me, it is my husband, daughter, and many friends, too numerous to list all here. I salute each of you for being my cheering squad and for reminding me that a dream is only a dream if you let it stay in your mind.

My husband, Albert, was more than my loyal supporter, he was my SME—faithfully guiding me with his insights and sharing his personal experiences. The best "first" husband any wife would be proud to call her own. Thank you, with all of my heart. I love you, always.

Julie, our daughter, continued to work her magic with designing a cover for this book that fittingly is a tribute to Marine's final story. The loss of dear Miloh, your dog of eight years, still stings. However, the memory of him will live on forever in our hearts. We will cherish him giving his love as he lay patiently under your desk waiting to go play while you worked. He knew you were doing important work for his granny. Thank you, Julie, for your "fiery" book designs and for sharing Miloh with your mom and dad. We love you, dearly.

How does one capture in a short sentence or two the value of a friend—Rosa Lee Jude—Thank you! If you've not enjoyed Rosa's stories, what are you waiting for? Find her stories and more of how to connect with her through her website: RosaLeeJude.com

The beta readers—Connie Martin, Marcella Taylor, and Carole Bybee—helped to make this series stellar! Their suggestions, questions, and eagle eyes helped me to become a better writer, and I am grateful!

A Time for Fire

To Donna Stroupe—a reader and editor who knows her commas—Thank you for helping to improve my story with your cleaver insights.

To my friends and friends to be, thank you for being readers of my words. Moreover, thank you for writing and connecting with me to let me know if I've touched your life in some small way.

There are so many more who offer support, please know I thank you very much.

Write on!

ABOUT THE AUTHOR

Pam B. Newberry lives in the mountains of Southwest Virginia with her husband where she is at work on her next series. The author of *The Letter: A Page of My Life*, *The Fire Within*, *The Fire of Revenge*, and *A Time for Fire*. She enjoys fun in the sun—gardening, fishing, and working with her husband on their hobby farm with their beloved honeybees.

Become a **Happy V. I. P. Reader** through her website: http://pambnewberry.com

Made in the USA
Charleston, SC
20 October 2015